NO ESCAPE

Ben Caywood walked slowly in the dark woods, until his foot caught on something heavy. He fell with a grunt—knowing as he did that what he'd fallen over was made of flesh. He hopped to his feet, his heart hammering, fumbling for the matches in his pocket to see what was on the ground. Hands trembling, he struck one. . . .

The light flared across a face intimately familiar, the face that had smiled down on him his entire life. The face of his father. He was dead, and on his chest was a piece of paper that carried the words—the same words laid upon the corpses of other Caywoods by the unseen killer in the woods.

Terror overwhelmed Ben Caywood. He turned, running blindly in the direction of the road that skirted the south edge of the forest. And even as he ran, he knew he was not alone.

Someone was behind him, pursuing him, and drawing nearer by the moment. . . .

Caywood Valley Feud

JUDSON GRAY

A SIGNET BOOK

SIGNET
Published by New American Library, a division of
Penguin Putnam Inc., 375 Hudson Street,
New York, New York 10014, U.S.A.
Penguin Books Ltd, 80 Strand,
London WC2R 0RL, England
Penguin Books Australia Ltd, Ringwood,
Victoria, Australia
Penguin Books Canada Ltd, 10 Alcorn Avenue,
Toronto, Ontario, Canada M4V 3B2
Penguin Books (N.Z.) Ltd, 182–190 Wairau Road,
Auckland 10, New Zealand

Penguin Books Ltd, Registered Offices:
Harmondsworth, Middlesex, England

First published by Signet, an imprint of New American Library,
a division of Penguin Putnam Inc.

First Printing, July 2002
10 9 8 7 6 5 4 3 2 1

Copyright © Cameron Judd, 2002

All rights reserved

 REGISTERED TRADEMARK—MARCA REGISTRADA

Printed in the United States of America

To Fred Brown,
journalist, author, and Tennessean

Prologue

The Caywood Valley, Arkansas

He wondered which would give out first, his
heart or his legs. He'd been running, dodg-
ing, hiding for nearly an hour now, and even
when he had not been in motion, pure fear had
kept his heart hammering and his lungs heaving.

He was determined not to be the next one. He
would not die as the others had, slaughtered in
the remoteness of these wooded hills, left to be
food for ants and worms and possums and birds.

Left to be found with a note mockingly written
in his own blood . . .

Not me, he thought. He would escape somehow, and get back to the safety of his home.

In the descending twilight he darted up one
more slope, found a tangle of fallen logs, and
dropped behind them. Never in his life had he
run so fast and hard. His chest throbbed beneath
his shirt.

He listened, praying that somehow he had

evaded his relentless pursuer. Hope began to rise. He heard nothing.

Still, he dared not leave his hiding place. His foe might be out there, waiting for him to appear.

If so, the murdering devil would wait for a long time. Ben Caywood would hide here all night, if he had to. He would remain awake, his pistol in his hand, his last two bullets still in the cylinder.

He would use those bullets carefully. He would not waste them. To do so would be to leave himself defenseless against his pursuer.

Time went by. The darkness thickened and Ben felt increasingly alone. Something his aunt had said, a dark speculation about the killer that haunted these Ozark hills, began to whisper at him from the back of his mind. He ignored it. He could not afford to let himself begin believing in ghosts. Not tonight.

Another hour passed. It was too dark to see anything now. He could leave, he felt sure, and not encounter the watching man. Maybe he wasn't even watching anymore. How could he, in so deep a night?

Ben Caywood stood slowly, trying to make no noise but not fully succeeding. Yet he heard nothing to make him think he was not alone.

He breathed deeply and stepped out into the forest. It was so dark he moved by touch rather than sight. Getting home would take a long time, but he had to try. He would not let his kin wonder where he was, not with all that had happened.

He had advanced only a hundred more yards when his foot caught on something heavy, pliant. He fell with a grunt, and knew as he did that what he'd fallen across was made of flesh.

Ben Caywood came to his feet with his heart hammering again. He stood frozen, wondering if what lay at his feet was animal or human. He had matches in his pocket . . . dare he strike one? Might the man who had pursued him still be nearby and see the flame?

But he had to know. He would let the flame flare for only a moment, just long enough to see.

Hands trembling, he pulled his matches from his pocket. He knelt, struck one. . . .

The light flared across a face infinitely familiar, the face that had smiled down on him in the earliest of his memories. The face of his father.

He was dead, and lying on his chest was a piece of paper with words scrawled upon it. He did not have time to read them, but it was unnecessary. He knew the words. They were the same ones laid upon the corpses of other Caywoods, slain in the same way by the same unseen murderer.

Terror overwhelmed him. He turned and ran blindly in the direction of the road that skirted the south edge of the forest. And as he ran, he knew for certain that he was not alone.

Someone was behind him, pursuing again, and drawing nearer by the moment.

Part I

---◆◆◆---

Into the Hills

Chapter One

Martin Pike advanced slowly along the oak floor of the general mercantile store, fingers flexing near the butt of the pistol holstered on his right hip. His gray eyes stared without blinking at Jim McCutcheon, who stood at the rear of the store, staring back, unsmiling.

"Looks like I've finally got you where I want you, McCutcheon," Pike said in a growling voice.

"Looks like it," McCutcheon replied.

Pike looked McCutcheon up and down. "You got no pistol today."

"There's a law against carrying pistols in this town. I'm a law-abiding man."

"Not me."

"So you'd gun a man down in cold blood?"

Pike smiled and slowly unbuckled his gunbelt, and let it and the pistol it held drop to the floor at his feet.

McCutcheon smiled tightly. "So it's fists, man to man."

"Fists are all I need to handle you."

McCutcheon gestured for Pike to come on. And Pike did, running toward Jim McCutcheon with all the speed a pair of six-year-old legs could muster.

Kneeling and letting the boy run into his arms, McCutcheon swept him up, both of them laughing. McCutcheon feigned a quick wrestling match, then collapsed to the floor like a man thoroughly beaten.

Emily Pike, Martin's mother, had walked through the front door moments before, watched the playful encounter, and broken into a laugh.

"I swear, sometimes I can't tell which of you is the boy and which is the man," she said.

McCutcheon came to his feet. "Why, Emily, you're looking mighty pretty today. What are you out and about for?"

She advanced toward McCutcheon, glanced around to make sure no one else was in the store, then planted a big kiss on his lips. "I'm just coming to see the man I'll marry a month from today."

"A month! Lordy! Is it really that close?"

"According to the calendar."

"I can hardly believe it."

"You don't sound very happy about it."

"Why, you know I'm happy. It's just that a month seems so long to wait."

She laughed. "You don't fool me, Jim McCutcheon. You're as nervous as a cat in a roomful of rocking chairs. But it's a good thing for me that we've still got a month. There's so much to do. A wedding is a big event in a lady's life."

He pondered silently that she would know better than most how important a wedding was, having been through one once already. That union that had been doomed from the start. The best thing to come out of it, she had told Mc-Cutcheon, was the birth of little Martin.

The divorce had been scandalous in the small Texas town. But better the scandal, she believed, than the miserable life she would have lived had the marriage remained intact. She and her former husband had both been young, naive, not ready for life as a married couple. It just hadn't worked out. After the divorce, she'd reverted to her maiden name and had her son's name changed to Pike as well.

"I ordered your suit today," she said.

"Oh. That's good."

She grinned slyly. "Good, my eye! I know you dread wearing that suit."

"Me and wool suits don't mix. They make me itch."

"Dear, you said that incorrectly. Don't say, 'Me and suits don't mix.' Say, 'Suits and I don't mix.' "

"You're pickier than a schoolmarm!"

"I used to be a schoolmarm, remember?" She gave his arm a squeeze. "Jim, I'm sorry if I'm too particular with you about your speech. I just know how important it is that a man of business present himself well. Speaking correctly is a big part of presenting a successful front to the world."

"In Texas? Where the drawls are so thick you can slice them like bread?"

"Are you always going to be so argumentative, husband?"

"Husband-to-be."

"However you label it, the point is, you're mine. And if all goes as it should, we'll be moving to Whitefield to operate Father's new store. I don't want Father deciding you have too much drawl to make the right kind of impression as a business partner."

"You worry too much."

"I worry just the right amount." And she hugged him.

He chuckled.

"What are you laughing at?"

"Just thinking how funny life is. It wasn't that long ago that I was out roaming the country with Jake Penn. Now I'm a merchant, about to be running a new store, and I've got a wife-to-be—even a son-to-be."

"Do you ever miss the roaming life?" she asked.

"What is there to miss about sleeping in the rain, scrabbling for a living any way I could get it, and feeling lucky to have a roof above me two or three times a month?"

"Nothing I can think of."

"Listen, honey, I've got work to finish up here. Is William back from Whitefield yet?"

"No. It may be supper time or later before he gets here. That's what he told Mother."

William Pike was Emily's father and McCutcheon's employer and future business partner. Pike had gone to the town of Whitefield to make a final decision regarding a building he hoped to buy or lease to house the mercantile establishment he wanted McCutcheon to manage for him there. "Maybe he'll come over to my place and tell me how things went."

"I'm sure he will."

"You come, too."

"I can't, Jim. I've got the Women's Missionary Support Society over at church tonight."

"Oh. I'd forgotten."

"I'll see you tomorrow, though."

"Good. And bring the little gunfighter back with you when you do." He poked gently at little Martin's thin shoulder. The boy growled at him, yanked out the hammerless, homemade revolver that he carried around in a crude leather gun belt his grandfather had made for him, and imitated the sound of a pistol firing.

McCutcheon grabbed at his chest, groaned, and staggered.

"Jim, you know I don't like you encouraging Martin to pretend he's shooting people. In fact, I don't like it that he carries around a gun at all."

"Honey, that's no gun. That's a hunk of metal that you couldn't shoot any more than if it was a piece of firewood."

"I don't like violence. Even the make-believe kind."

McCutcheon had to sympathize. He'd seen enough violence during his time with Jake Penn to last him for the rest of his days.

"I'll quit going on with him about the fighting and shooting, if that's what you want."

"It is."

McCutcheon sighed softly, then winked at Martin. "Looks like you and me have to make a permanent peace, Kid Pike."

"Yeah. Lucky for you. I'd a whupped you."

"Martin, that's not proper speech," Emily declared.

McCutcheon laughed. "See you tomorrow. Both of you."

He tousled Martin's hair and gave Emily a kiss on the cheek.

Chapter Two

Technically, the house was rented, but Mc-Cutcheon had not paid rent for the last three months. The place belonged to his future father-in-law, and nothing was expected from Mc-Cutcheon except that he simply live there. After the wedding, Emily would join him here until the planned move to Whitefield—assuming the business side of the matter all worked out. If it didn't, they would stay here permanently, Mc-Cutcheon still working in the store like he did now.

He sat now on the long, covered porch, looking down across the southern end of town and into the darkening plains beyond. He sipped a strong cup of coffee—which he hoped would not keep him awake later—and puffed on a mild cigar he had pilfered from the jar at the store. The pilferage, like the failure to pay rent, was an offense ignored. McCutcheon had discovered that life is easy when you are engaged to marry the daughter of your boss and landlord.

He was in a mellow mood tonight, a frame of mind much more common to him now that he was no longer a drifter. Not until he had settled down had he come to realize just how precarious life had been while in the company of footloose Jake Penn. Seldom a creature comfort, seldom a hot meal on a table—or for that matter, a table at all—and usually nothing beyond spare change in his pocket. In retrospect he could see how hard it really had been. This was much better.

It was the Blain affair down at the border, and beyond into Mexico, that had made the difference. When the niece of wealthy rancher Abel Blain had been kidnapped, and the job of carrying the ransom had fallen in large part to Penn and McCutcheon, a grateful Abel Blain had paid both men generously. For the first time since he had squandered away his inheritance, McCutcheon had found himself situated to make something of his life.

The obtaining of this instant wealth had led to newfound ventures. He and Jake had separated: McCutcheon deciding to use his money to find a new, settled life; Penn using his to finance his continued quest to locate his long-missing sister.

It hadn't been easy to dissolve a partnership as strong as theirs had become. But Penn had insisted on it. The money was a chance for McCutcheon to change his life. The young man shouldn't miss out on it.

Here in this little but thriving town of Sweetbush, Texas, McCutcheon had found the opportunity he needed. He'd gone to work for William Pike, general mercantile merchant, and not just because Pike's lovely and unmarried daughter had immediately caught his eye. An additional allure of this place had been simple American commerce and the new hope it gave him for his future.

Emily Pike had grown on him very quickly, a process in no way hindered by the fact that her father so obviously favored the relationship. Before long, Jim McCutcheon, so recently a common wanderer, found himself not only a businessman, but an engaged one. The scandal of Emily's divorce was not a problem for McCutcheon. He'd never been one to care much about what other people thought.

McCutcheon propped his feet up on the porch railing and tilted his chair back, looking down the street toward the white, steepled church where he and Emily would be married in a month. He found it difficult to envision the ceremony. As excited as he was at the prospect of marriage, he had been a loner for so long that he could barely imagine himself any other way.

McCutcheon noticed someone striding up the street in his direction.

"Good evening, Jim."

"Hello, William. How did it go today in Whitefield?"

"Excellent. I worked out a lease. The location, the building . . . perfect for us."

McCutcheon nodded. "Good. I've been thinking about it all day."

William Pike stepped up onto the porch and sat down in the empty rocking chair beside McCutcheon. In his left hand was a folded newspaper, in his right a pie tin with half an apple pie in it. McCutcheon eyed the latter.

William handed it to him. "I brought this over from the house. Lucy baked it for supper, and she thought you might like to have some. Here. There's a fork already in it. And I brought you a paper from Whitefield. I've done read it, so you can have it."

"Bless Lucy's heart," McCutcheon said, taking both the pie and newspaper. He set the pie in his lap and the paper on the floor beside his rocker. The news could wait. The pie demanded instant attention.

"Lucy is the queen of apple pies," William said. "It's why I married her."

McCutcheon dug out a forkful and thrust it into his mouth. He chewed with deep satisfaction.

"Makes you glad to be marrying into the family?"

"Indeed."

"Jim, I just can't be more pleased about how things are working out. As you know, Lucy and I have held a deep concern for Emily and Martin's welfare ever since her ... uh, her ..."

"Divorce."

"Yes."

McCutcheon gathered more pie on his fork. He wondered why it was so difficult for people to talk about divorce. Even Emily herself could hardly discuss it with him.

"I believe you are going to be good for Emily and Martin both. And I believe you'll be good for the business as well. You strike me as level-headed, not the kind to make rash or hasty decisions."

McCutcheon could have laughed. He had made more than his share of hasty, rash decisions in his time. He had squandered his family inheritance and taken up life as a drifter, drinking and brawling and cursing at the world rather than applying himself to rebuilding his lost fortune. Only the fortuitous circumstance of the Blain reward money he and Jake Penn had earned down at the border had enabled him to quit drifting. But he wasn't about to describe past failures to a man destined to be his father-in-law.

William Pike went on. "Emily needs a good, settled husband. And Lord knows Martin needs a father since his real one isn't around anymore. He needs the kind of man who will be there when he needs him, setting the right kind of example in the way he lives his life. You know, I can already see Martin as an excellent man of business someday. Even at his age, there are traits that show through. We need to encourage these things. To let him see that a man is at his best when he controls himself, when he keeps himself with his nose to the grindstone."

"Yes. As long as there's time for him to be a boy, too," Jim said.

Pike paused a few moments to dig out his pipe and tobacco pouch. When he was lighted up and puffing, he shook out his match and said, "So, Jim, are you looking forward to married life?"

"Yes, sir."

William stretched and yawned. "I tell you, Jim. Life can sure change a man's course. There you were, wandering around the country, and now you're all settled down and ready to marry."

"Yes, sir."

"Do you miss your roaming life?"

The truth was, at times, McCutcheon did. Parts of it, anyway. But he'd not say so to William. "Actually, I was talking to Emily today about how much better life is now."

This was what William wanted to hear. He smiled and nodded. "Who was that fellow you roamed with?"

McCutcheon tensed. There were things he

hadn't said about Jake—one thing in particular, because he suspected what William's reaction might be. "His name is Jake Penn."

"And he's looking for a sister, you said?"

"That's right."

"Interesting. How did they come to be apart?"

This was cutting too close to an uncomfortable area. "They were separated as children."

"You've told me that much before. But how did it happen?"

McCutcheon made a quick decision. Time for the truth. Might as well find out once and for all how the family he was about to marry into would react to knowing he had been partnered with a black man. "They were separated when they were both still slaves."

Silence. William looked at him as if he'd not heard right.

"What did you say?"

"Slaves. They were slaves."

Another long pause. "So Jake Penn is a . . . Negro?"

"That's right."

William looked away, frowning. "You roamed around the country as the partner of a *Negro*."

"I did."

William fidgeted in his chair, frowning into the night.

McCutcheon had been afraid of this. There had been subtle indications before that William held a low view of the formerly enslaved race, but McCutcheon had held out hope that he was misinterpreting the man. Apparently not.

"Did you have too hard a time of it, running around with a darky?"

"No. I liked being with Jake. I didn't think about him in terms of his color. Jake Penn was always just Jake Penn, a good man."

"But . . . a black one."

"Yes. That's true."

William Pike shook his head. "I can't imagine doing that, don't think that I could stand to keep company with a black man that long. Especially if he had the notion of himself as my equal."

McCutcheon felt a burst of anger. He set the pie tin down on the porch beside him and began to rock rather violently, trying to keep his calm. It wouldn't pay to fly off the handle with his future father-in-law.

He wondered in a momentary flash of worry if William's racism had rubbed off on Emily.

William began to silently brood and began rocking in tandem with McCutcheon. He reached down, picked up the newspaper he had brought, rolled it into a tight stick and slapped at his own knee repeatedly with it. McCutcheon quickly found this annoying.

"Any good reading in that paper?" he finally asked, eager to move the conversation onto more comfortable terrain.

"Here. Read it for yourself and make your own decision." William's tone was snappish. He stood abruptly as he tossed the paper into Mc-Cutcheon's lap. "Think I'll head back to the house. Keep the pie tin for now. You can give it back later."

McCutcheon watched William Pike stalk away.

This didn't bode well. He wondered how William would react if he ever learned the *full* truth: that the McCutcheon family had been active in the Underground Railroad before the war. How would he respond if he found out that the first time McCutcheon had met Jake Penn, Mc-Cutcheon had been a mere boy and Penn had been a slave fleeing north to Canada?

Maybe he should have just kept his mouth shut this evening and maintained the peace. But that wouldn't have been possible forever. One of these days, Jake Penn would come riding into town to visit his old partner, and the truth would come out.

And, blast it, why should he hide the salient facts about Jake Penn, just because one man was too bigoted to deal with them? This was William's problem, not McCutcheon's.

McCutcheon decided to cast aside serious thoughts for the moment and take refuge in apple pie and a fresh newspaper.

The pie first. He finished it, set the plate aside,

and picked up the newspaper. He scooted his chair closer to the window to catch light from the lamp inside.

The paper was the weekly out of Whitefield, and most of the news was local to that town and of little interest to McCutcheon. He scanned a few columns and examined the advertisements. He looked for national stories, state news. His rocker creaked loudly.

He flipped a page, and the rocker stopped. McCutcheon stared at the headline near the bottom of the penultimate page:

MYSTERIOUS NEGRO KILLER PLAGUES OZARK FAMILY WITH DEATH AND DESTRUCTION.

Beneath it, a subhead:

PHANTOM MURDERER'S GRIM NOTES SAY HE WIELDS DEATH IN "VENGEANCE FOR NORA."

Nora was the name of Jake Penn's sister.

Chapter Three

McCutcheon pulled the paper close to his face, straining to read in the dim light. The story was remarkable, and chilling.

The family's name was Caywood. The Ozark clan was depicted by the unidentified writer of the story as successful farmers, livestock and horse traders, and hunters—self-reliant, rugged individualists typical of the mountains. The patriarch was one Macnamara Caywood, a man of relatively high wealth but failing health.

The Caywood family had a most unusual problem. For several months, members of the clan had been turning up dead in remote, wooded areas. Generally, the victims, all males so far, had died from gunshots. One had been stabbed. The exact number of those killed so far was unknown to the writer of the story.

Notes had been found with each of the victims, usually written on scraps of paper pinned to their collars:

VENGEANCE FOR NORA.

Who is Nora? the story queried. *Though the Caywood family will not speak to the matter publicly, others in the vicinity declare that Nora was a Negro woman who suffered a great wrong many years ago, apparently at the hands of the Caywoods. The precise nature of this alleged crime and the exact perpetrator of it, are facts that are notoriously difficult to ascertain.*

Chief among the legends, however, is one that alleges the killing of Nora by a member of the Caywood clan. A man related to the unfortunate woman, it is said, vowed upon his own death to return as a phantom and avenge her. Thus the predominating explanation of this strange Ozarks story turns out to be a typical mountain ghost tale. There are those who find this mysterious explanation satisfying, but others who see a more flesh-and-blood killer upon the loose, and attach to these strange events the influence of another family of the same vicinity, who, it is said, has been at odds with the Caywoods for many years.

McCutcheon read on to the story's end, then read the entire thing one more time. He folded the paper, laid it on the porch beside him, and stared across the dark street.

He did not like the thoughts running through his head just now.

* * *

William Pike seemed more his usual self the next morning. He said nothing about the prior night or about Jake Penn.

Even so, the day was not a good one for Mc-Cutcheon. That newspaper story—now clipped and saved in his pocket—weighed on his mind. He told himself that Jake Penn would never do the kind of things the story described. Jake was no murderer. McCutcheon couldn't imagine Jake ambushing a man and leaving him dead in some Ozark hollow with a note pinned to his collar.

But might he do so if that man had brought harm to his beloved Nora?

No. Not even for Nora would Jake become a murderer. McCutcheon couldn't let himself believe it.

Yet the questions lingered, growing heavier as the day wore on. When Emily and Martin came by in the afternoon, McCutcheon found it was all he could do to make himself pay attention to them.

Two days later

Emily Pike looked worriedly at Jim McCutcheon, who was busily sweeping out the back room of the store. He worked with an odd intensity and a frown that concerned her.

What was wrong with him? For that matter, what was wrong with her father, who had also had a different manner for a couple of days? Come to think of it, her father's odd behavior had been noticeable only when McCutcheon was present.

She glanced at Martin, who was happily playing in the corner with a hammer he had taken from the tool shelf. He was oblivious to the tensions around him, but it was all beginning to nag at her nerves more than she could take. With a firm pursing of her lips, Emily decided to get an answer right now. She walked toward McCutcheon determinedly.

"Jim, I want to talk to you," she said.

He looked up at her. "Surely. Is something wrong?"

"That's what I want to ask *you*. Tell me what's bothering you."

"What makes you think anything is bothering me?"

"How can I think anything else? You've been moping around for two days."

"Well . . . with the wedding coming up, and all the plans about us opening a store . . . I just got a lot on my mind."

"'I just have a lot on my mind.' That's how you should say it. But there's more to it than that, I think. You seem like a different person, and it worries me."

"I'm not a different person. I'm just myself."

"I know you well enough to know when something is wrong. I've been watching you sweep that floor like you're trying to wear a hole through it. Tell me what's on your mind!"

He laid the broom aside and looked at her closely. "Have you noticed that your father has been a little . . . distant to me lately?"

She knitted her brows. "I've noticed he's been a bit grouchy."

"Yes. It stems from a conversation we had two nights back."

"What conversation?"

McCutcheon looked around the store. No one else was here, other than Martin. This was as good a time as any to tell her what he had told William.

"Two nights back, right after your father came back, he and I talked on the porch of my house. I told him something about Jake Penn that he hadn't known . . . and that you don't know, either."

She looked scared. "What?"

"I told him that Jake Penn is a black man."

She looked at him oddly, smiled, then laughed. "Are you joking with me? You are, aren't you?"

"Why would you think I'm joking?"

She actually backed away from him a step. "Jim! Why would you do such a thing?"

"Do what? Spend time with a Negro?"

"Not just spend time! I've heard you say more than once that Jake Penn was your partner. You treated him as an equal."

"Good Lord, Emily, he *is* my equal! And yours! A man is a man. That's how I was brought up. Jake Penn was my friend and partner. What color his skin is don't matter."

"Jim, you talk like some kind of . . . I don't know, reformer, or some old abolitionist."

"I favored the abolitionists, Emily. You may as well know it. My family even . . ." He faltered. He'd been about to reveal his family's participation in the Underground Railroad. But doing so might cost him more than he wanted to pay just now.

"Your family what?"

"Just suffice it to say they thought different about such things than your father does . . . different than you, too, I guess."

After a long pause and obvious struggle, she forced out a rather ghastly-looking smile. "Well . . . I suppose it doesn't really matter now, does it? I mean, you're not doing it anymore. Now you're with me."

"That's right."

She hugged him. It was a stiffer, more forced hug than usual.

He hugged her back, just as stiffly.

"Come over for supper tonight," she said.

"You sure?"

"Yes. Mother is expecting you."

"All right."

She hugged him again, turned, and called to Martin. They left Jim McCutcheon alone in the store.

He retrieved his broom and leaned on it a few moments, very depressed. It was amazing to him that something so unimportant as the mere fact he had been a close friend of a black man mattered so much to the Pike family.

If that meager detail knocked them so far off kilter, he couldn't imagine how they'd respond when he told them what he had decided to do.

He pulled from his pocket the torn-out article from the newspaper William had given him, and quickly reread its account of the phantom killer in the Ozarks. Despite his attempts to argue himself out of the notion, he couldn't shake off the idea that what was going on had something to do with Jake Penn.

Vengeance for Nora.

There was only one way to find the answer, and the whole prospect filled him with the greatest dread.

He'd have to tell her soon. Tonight, he decided. After supper. He couldn't tell her all of it.
But what part he would tell her, he hoped she'd
find some way to understand.

Chapter Four

Two days later

The train stood steaming and hissing, ready to pull out of the station and begin its long journey toward Arkansas.

McCutcheon's roan was already ensconced in the stable car, his tack gear was safely locked up in cargo storage, and his ticket was in his pocket.

McCutcheon stood with his bag at his feet and his hands in his pockets, looking sadly at Emily's tear-stained face. She stood three feet from him, not willing to draw nearer, which troubled him. Little Martin was not present, being back at his grandparents' house, too upset by McCutcheon's departure to join his mother in seeing him off.

"I can't understand this," Emily said. "I'm to be your wife. We have important business changes looming that mean Father needs you here. But here you are, getting ready to leave for Arkansas for reasons you won't even tell me."

"I wish I could tell you," McCutcheon said.

"Truly I do." But how could he possibly reveal that he was leaving his family-to-be to head into the Arkansas wilderness to find out if an alleged black-skinned murderer roaming the Ozark hills was his old friend and partner?

"Jim, at least be honest enough to tell me if you're running away from me. If you are having second thoughts about marrying me—"

"It's not that, Emily. It isn't, I promise." Yet he wasn't sure now that this was fully the truth. The initial impetus toward Arkansas was the matter involving the killer in the mountains, but now that he knew his fiancée shared the bigoted views of her father, he wondered if that, too, had become an added motivation for this flight. Maybe he was having second thoughts after all.

"Then tell me if you're doing this for yourself, or someone else."

He paused. "For someone else."

"A man or woman?"

"A man."

She looked relieved for a moment, but then her face grew stern again. "Jake Penn?"

This caught him off guard. How could she know? "Yes," he said after a moment.

She withdrew from him a half step, clearly surprised, and he realized she hadn't known at all. "You're abandoning me and Martin and your obligations here for the sake of some old drifting Negro who can't let go of the past."

"Jake Penn is my friend. And I have reason to think he might be in the midst of a bad situation."

"What makes you think so?"

He would not tell her about what he had read in the newspaper. "I can't really say."

He could see that she disbelieved him. She was perceiving this trip as a feeble and contrived excuse for a flight from marriage, and he couldn't blame her.

She put out her hand. "Good-bye, Jim. I hope I'll see you again. I hope you don't breech your vow to me."

He was not willing to part this way. He went to her and put his arms around her, sweeping her to him. He kissed her firmly and would not let go of her. It troubled him to feel her stiffening, resisting him. "I will be back. And I'll marry you and become a father to Martin. And whatever you may think of what I'm doing, be assured that if I wasn't doing it, I would be less of a husband for you and less of a father for Martin. I'm doing something that is right and necessary, and all I can do is ask you to believe me."

"Just tell me why you are going."

He almost did, but one thing kept him from it. It was important to him that his wife accept Jake Penn. Already she disliked Jake because of his race and because she viewed him as a sort of competitor for McCutcheon's attention and devotion. He couldn't tell her that he feared Jake had turned into a murderer. It would only further guarantee her hatred of him.

"When it's through, maybe I can tell you then."

He sensed her struggle, but was relieved when her body relaxed a little. She leaned into his arms and kissed him again.

"Good-bye, Jim," she said, beginning to weep. She pulled away and scurried off, not looking back at him. He started to call to her—but didn't.

The conductor yelled his all-aboard call. Feeling sadder than he had felt in many a year, Jim McCutcheon watched Emily vanish around the train station platform, sighed, picked up his bag, and boarded the train.

He was grimly thoughtful the full extent of the journey. He shunned the efforts of other passengers to engage him in conversation, paid scant attention to the passing landscape, and found himself unable to think long on any subjects but his family-to-be back home and the matter of Jake Penn that lay ahead. Assuming it was Jake Penn he would find. He hoped it wouldn't be. He didn't want Jake to have turned into a killer.

He was asleep when the train rolled to the last stop of his journey. The lurching as the brakes engaged and the bustle of the passengers preparing to disembark stirred Jim awake. He rubbed

his eyes and stood, picking up his bag and glancing out the window at the remarkably beautiful
country to which he'd come.

It was early autumn, and the hills were turning spectacular hues of russet, gold, and brilliant
orange. The country here reminded McCutcheon
in many ways of the kind of terrain he had
grown up in, and he was struck by an unexpected burst of loneliness, suddenly missing his
parents, dead now for several years. He missed
Emily, too, and wished he was still in Texas.

"Pardon me, sir."

McCutcheon turned. One of the crewmen of
the train was approaching.

"Yes, sir?"

"Is your name McCutcheon?"

"Yes. James McCutcheon."

"Uh, yes." The man seemed ill at ease. "That's
your roan in the stable car, then."

"Yes. I was just heading there to get it. Why?"

"Uh, I'm afraid your horse is sick."

"Sick?"

"Yes. We had just got it off the train when it
simply collapsed."

McCutcheon headed toward the stable car at a
trot. A little crowd of men was gathered around
his horse, which lay on its side, breathing heavily
and jerkily.

McCutcheon pushed through and knelt, looking at the stricken animal.

"Your horse, young man?" asked a burly, be-spectacled man with a somber manner and shoe-brush mustache.

"Yes."

"Well, I'm sorry to tell you, but your horse is dying."

"I can see that. What happened?"

"Heart, I think. I raise horses. I've had two do this within the last four years. That horse is a goner. Sorry."

McCutcheon stood, shaking his head. He felt more upset than he was willing to show. "It's a shame. That's been a fine horse. A little old, but always strong. I had no idea it had a bad heart."

"It's the same with horses as with people. You can't always tell."

McCutcheon scratched at the back of his neck, unsure what to do.

"If you want, son, I'll take care of easing its suffering for you. It's the best thing."

"Not yet . . . maybe it's not its heart. Maybe it will get up in a minute."

He'd just finished saying it when the horse gave a great shudder, made an odd, faint whinny, and ceased to breathe. McCutcheon saw the light go out of its eyes.

"Well, so much for that," the horse-raiser said. "Sorry, young man."

Others in the group muttered their own condolences. McCutcheon hid his distress and sadness. He'd been fond of this horse.

It was also a very inconvenient loss. McCutcheon had counted on riding this horse into the mountains. Now he had no means of transport other than his feet, and there was the matter of having to dispose of the dead animal besides.

Conveniently, a man who had been observing all this from the seat of a wagon over near the train station climbed down from his perch and walked up to the group.

"Pardon me, sir," he said to McCutcheon, "but I know a feller not a mile from here who buys dead horses and cattle and such."

McCutcheon asked, "How do I find him?"

"You don't need to. I'll go get him . . . if you're willing to sell him the horse."

McCutcheon was in no mood for commerce. "Tell you what—if he's willing to take care of it for me, he can have it for free."

The man nodded enthusiastically. "He'll take that bargain, sir. I can vouch for that because he's my brother. Have you got a saddle to sell, too?"

"No. I suppose I'll have to buy me another horse."

"I know a man who can sell you one, cheap."

"How many brothers you got? Thanks, but for now I don't want to fool with it. I just want some supper and a place to spend the night."

Chapter Five

Jim ate his supper slowly, there being no reason to rush what was bound to be the highlight of his evening. He'd already checked into the only hotel in this backwater community of Fitch, Arkansas. The hotel was a flea-bag two-story building with drafty rooms and a floor that sagged so badly that everything that wasn't square rolled toward one side of the room.

If he was lucky, he would stay in his room alone. The proprietor had already warned him that the arrival of another male guest would give him a bedmate. McCutcheon hoped nobody else would appear.

Now he sat in a small café across the street from his hotel. The food was good, the coffee better. McCutcheon ate a slab of apple pie for dessert—certainly not as good as Mrs. Pike's—then lingered over the coffee while he smoked a cigar. The sun set over hills, its beauty fading with the light.

McCutcheon fought dejection. This whole venture now seemed ludicrous. One questionable newspaper article, and he'd endangered his engagement and his business future to come here to a strange place to chase a mere suspicion. How did he know that the newspaper story wasn't pure fiction?

And now his horse was dead. It was going so badly that it was almost funny. But not quite.

The door creaked open and the fattest man McCutcheon had ever seen lumbered in, wheezing with every step. McCutcheon couldn't help but stare. To his surprise, the man looked straight over at him, turned with some obvious effort, and waddled his way. Four hundred pounds, McCutcheon figured, and surely not a pound less.

The man stopped and gazed down at McCutcheon through the slits in his face that served for eyes.

"You're setting where I set," the man said.

"What?"

"I always set in that chair when I eat here."

McCutcheon glared at the man. "So this table belongs to you?"

Seeing what was happening, the man who ran the place rushed up, wiping his hands on a white cloth. "Pardon me, sir," he said to McCutcheon, "you may be taking Cletus wrong. He does sit there every time he eats here, but it's only because that chair you're in is one we strengthened especially for him."

"Oh. I see." McCutcheon's annoyance faded.

"Cletus broke five, six chairs before we figured out we were going to have to fix him something special, you see. So we strengthened up that chair. Take a look at it."

McCutcheon did. Metal bars had been fixed to the legs. "I'll be."

"There's a metal plate under the seat, too."

McCutcheon crushed out his cigar. "So there is. I'm finished, anyway. You can have your chair, Mr. Cletus."

"You ain't got to go. Just let me set in that chair and you can set in the one 'cross from me."

"Cletus likes to have folks to talk to," the proprietor explained.

McCutcheon wasn't in the mood to talk. But he also didn't look forward to going to that louse-ridden hotel. Maybe he could handle a second piece of pie and a few minutes of conversation.

He moved to the other chair, and listened with some worry as the chair he had just vacated groaned and snapped loudly under Cletus's weight. But it held.

"The usual, Cletus?"

"Yeah."

"You got the money?" The proprietor then added, for McCutcheon's sake, "Cletus has to pay extra because he eats so much. He saves up for it."

"I see. Tell you what: another piece of pie for me," McCutcheon said.

McCutcheon's pie arrived much more quickly than Cletus' "usual," and Cletus watched with intense, jealous interest as his companion began to eat.

"Is it good today?"

"Yes."

"Pie here is always good. I usually eat one when I come."

"Do you? This is my second piece."

"I always eat a whole pie. Once I ate two of them."

McCutcheon would have doubted this claim if made by a lesser man than Cletus.

Cletus' plate arrived heavily laden, and conversation ceased for a time as the man dug into his victuals. The vigor and enthusiasm Cletus put into the act of devouring was unsettling and not very pleasant to see. But McCutcheon couldn't tear his eyes away. He was reduced to nibbling at his piecrust, his appetite now gone.

When Cletus finished the plateful he signaled for another. While awaiting it, he swiped his mouth with a napkin and studied McCutcheon a little more closely than before, not being quite so distracted by hunger.

"What's your name?" Cletus asked.

"Jim McCutcheon."

"Where you come from?"

"A lot of places. Texas, most recently."

"Yeah. Texas. I been over into Texas some."

The second plate was on its way now, as heavily laden as the first. "You traveling on business or pleasure?"

Nosy fellow, this Cletus. "Business. Personal. Not much pleasure to it."

"Ain't many folks can find business around here. Not much in these parts but cattle ranchers and farmers and piney hills." Cletus began eating with renewed gusto.

"I'm not staying here. I'm heading into the hills. An area called Caywood Valley."

Cletus stopped chewing and stared at Mc-Cutcheon, his eyes as wide as his facial puffiness would allow. "Why would you want to go there?"

"Well . . . there may be someone there who I know. I need to go see if it's really him."

"I'd stay out of them hills," Cletus said seriously. "A man goes in there, he may not come back out."

"Why?"

"The feud, for one thing! Ain't you heard about the feud?"

McCutcheon recalled a mention in the newspaper story of a family that had been at odds with the Caywoods for some years, but he wasn't aware of any full-fledged feud. "Tell me about it."

"The Caywoods and the Harpers. They've been shooting each other for so long nobody can remember when it started. It all started back in Kentucky, where both families came from years and years ago. And then danged if both families didn't wind up in the same stretch of Arkansas, and kept their fight going just like back home! The Harpers and Caywoods have always found something to hate and kill each other over."

"I hadn't heard about the feud," McCutcheon said. "But I'm not feuding with either family. They wouldn't just kill a man for being in their territory, surely."

"Maybe they would, maybe they wouldn't. Depends on what they think that man's business is. You got to watch out for the Caywoods. And even more for the Harpers. The Caywoods are the richer of the families, and the most settled. Folks say that Mack Caywood is a good man who would like to see the feud stop. But the Harpers are just plumb mean. Mountain kind of folks, who settled in the Ozarks God-only-knows how many years ago. A Harper will kill you if you so much as look at him cross-eyed. And right now I figure its worse than ever out in them hills—there's something more than just the feud to worry about."

McCutcheon could guess where this was

going, but decided to play ignorant. "What's that?"

Cletus leaned forward and lowered his voice. "There's somebody . . . or something . . . killing the Caywoods back in them hills. Picking them off one by one, and leaving notes on their corpses. And this killer ain't a Harper. Because the Harpers are white folks, and them who have caught a glimpse of this killer say he is a black man. If he's a man at all."

"What else would he be? It's hard to imagine a woman doing such things."

Cletus went back to eating again, talking while he chewed. McCutcheon tried not to look too closely. "Not a woman. But maybe a ghost. You believe in such things?"

"In my experience, it's always been living and breathing humans who kill other humans."

Cletus shook his head while he loaded his fork. "They say this killer, he's like a phantom. Come and go like a fog, and leaves no tracks. Them Caywoods have gone hunting for this killer like he was a varmint, and never found no sign of him. Then, a day or two later, there's another dead Caywood with another note around his neck."

McCutcheon stared off into the corner. "Jake was always able to vanish like a fog," he muttered to himself.

"What?"

"Nothing. Just thinking out loud."

Cletus stared hard at McCutcheon. "You don't know something about this killer, do you?"

"No. No, of course not. Though now that I hear your story, I do recollect reading something like that recently in a newspaper."

Cletus laughed, showing coated teeth and a mouth full of half-chewed food. "Oh, I know about that! Some newspaper writer come showing up, talking about going back into the hills to chase down a story about this killer, and when he heard the talk about it, that was the end of that! He listened to the rumors, wrote 'em all up, and never so much as set foot into the hills. But Jimmy gave him the straight story."

"Who's Jimmy?"

"Him over yonder, the one who runs this place. The same one who's been bringing the food."

McCutcheon looked over. Jimmy was watching and listening. When McCutcheon met his eye, Jimmy left the stool he'd been perched on and came to the table.

"Can I sit?"

McCutcheon motioned for him to join them. Jimmy grabbed a chair from a nearby table and scooted it in beside McCutcheon and Cletus.

"You fellows will pardon me for eavesdropping, I hope. Cletus is right. I did give that newspaperman the straight story. But things have changed since. This killer ain't just going after Caywoods no more. A couple of Harpers are dead, too."

"You don't mean it!" Cletus exclaimed, shifting in his chair and making it groan as if suffering.

"It's true. Two feuding families both being killed off by a lone man. And he leaves the same note on the corpses of Caywoods and Harpers alike. 'Vengeance for Nora.'"

"The story in the paper said that people believe the killer is avenging something done to a Negro woman years ago," McCutcheon said.

"People speculate everything," Jimmy replied. "Nobody really knows. All I can say is that it don't appear likely to me that such a tale is true now that he's killing Harpers right along with Caywoods.

"Are you a newspaper writer yourself?" Jimmy asked McCutcheon.

"No," McCutcheon replied. "My interest is purely private."

"I heard you say you were planning to go back into the mountains," Jimmy said seriously. "You shouldn't. It's dangerous back in there. Hell, it was dangerous even before this killer come along! Now it's worse. If he's killing Caywoods and Harpers both, who's to say he wouldn't kill anybody else who came along, too?"

"I don't have a choice but to go," McCutcheon

said. "I think a friend of mine may be back there. Maybe he's in trouble."

"Well, I can understand your thinking, no question about it. If I had a friend or relative back in those hills with all this going on, I'd want to go fetch them out, too. That killer could go after anybody."

Cletus had about finished his plate of food. A third was bound to follow. He scraped the dish with his fork, chasing straying peas.

"All I can say is, you'll not find me back in them hills," he said. "Not for nobody."

Jimmy eyed McCutcheon. "Cletus may be right. Just how important is this friend to you?"

McCutcheon thought about all the miles he and Jake Penn had roamed together. The dangers they had faced and endured together. The way Jake Penn had saved his life. "He's very important. I have no choice about it," he said.

"Then be careful, my friend. Be very careful."

"I will."

Cletus said, "I'm ready for another plate, Jimmy."

"You're going to bust one of these days, Cletus. Absolutely bust wide open. I'll have to turn the dogs in just to clean up the mess."

Now there was an image McCutcheon could do without. This was his cue to leave.

"Good evening, gentlemen," he said. "Thank you for the company, and the information."

"You be careful back in them hills, my friend," Jimmy said. "Be very careful."

Back at the hotel, McCutcheon encountered the closest thing to good news that the day had brought: No one else had appeared looking for lodging. The bed in his room would be his alone.

He smoked another cigar and thought about what he had left behind in Texas, and what lay ahead in the Ozark hills. The former he knew well; the latter he couldn't really guess. Probably he would wander into the hills, roam around, find nothing, and end up going back to Emily and Martin.

It couldn't be Jake committing those murders. Jake wouldn't kill wantonly, out of vengeance. It was inconceivable.

But those notes—"Vengeance for Nora." Who else but Jake would leave a note like that?

Vengeance . . . for what? If this was Jake's Nora, what had happened to her? It would have to be something terrible to make Jake turn to murder.

McCutcheon finished his cigar, put it out, and turned off the light. He rolled onto his side, feeling the tilt of the floor even in the bed. Eventually he slept.

Deep in the night, something moved in the room. McCutcheon sat up. A dark figure stood by his bed.

"Roll over," the figure said. "This bed's sleeping two the rest of the night."

McCutcheon groaned. Another lodger after all. Just his luck.

He rolled over, scooting to the other side of the bed. The bed heaved like a boat on turbulent water as the other man climbed in. A few minutes later heavy snoring filled the room.

McCutcheon lay there, unable to go back to sleep for an hour. At last he grew accustomed to the sawmill chorus rising beside him, and fell asleep again.

The man was gone when McCutcheon opened his eyes the next morning. So, too, was McCutcheon's bag, in which he had kept all his money except a few dollars he had transferred from his pocket to his boot just before he'd turned in. His pistol, rifle, and ammunition were still where he'd hidden them under the bed, but his extra clothing was in his missing bag.

He darted downstairs, hoping he might catch up to the thief. Finding no one around, he darted to the café. Jimmy was there, putting breakfast onto the table, but the thief was long gone.

McCutcheon swore beneath his breath. His horse was dead, almost all his money was stolen, and he was many miles from his Texas home and the woman he would marry.

If he had enough money left, he might just

buy himself a ticket home and put all this behind
him before even more bad luck came his way.

Jim McCutcheon didn't go home. Instead, he
arranged to have his saddle stored, and with
some of his meager remaining funds bought
himself a little supply of food and a cloth sack to
carry it in. McCutcheon went on his way with
the bag and his bedroll slung over one shoulder
and his rifle, now tied to a cord, strung over the
other. He'd come too far and gone through far
too many headaches and troubles to turn back
now.

He had a few dollars left, and his guns, and if
his horse was gone, he still had his own two legs,
and they were in working order. Besides, there
was the hope that he might stumble across the
man who had robbed him and get back what
he'd lost. This was a vague notion at best, one he
brought up to himself simply as a pretext for jus-
tifying what he knew he had to do, whether it
made sense or not. But it gave him enough motivation to move on into the hills, looking for Jake
Penn.

He thought back on a time Penn had come
looking for him, shortly after they had been separated after their first meeting with each other.
Penn had realized that the young good-for-
nothing was none other than the grown-up version of the boy member of a family who had

housed and hid him while he was a fleeing slave many years before. He'd doubled back to find McCutcheon literally swinging in a noose, lynched as a horse thief, and had saved his life.

There were still times, in just the right light, when McCutcheon could make out the faintest of scars left around his neck by that hangman's rope. Every time he saw it he was reminded of just how much he owed Jake Penn.

Trying not to dwell too much on the warnings he had received in the café, he moved ahead, following a wagon road that plunged deep into the hills. He began to consider the likely futility of this effort. If it did prove to be Jake Penn out haunting this wild Ozark wilderness, he would be in hiding, and Penn was a man no one would be able to find. And if it wasn't Penn out there, then finding whoever it was might be a fatal mistake. Penn wouldn't harm McCutcheon, surely, but a murderous stranger might.

McCutcheon decided not to think further about such things, and forged on.

Chapter Six

Even though there was no one around to know about it, it was hard on McCutcheon's pride to admit that he was lost.

The day was waning and McCutcheon had put many miles behind him. His legs ached from exertion, which made him miss his horse more than ever.

He had encountered only one other human being during his jaunt, and had taken a word of advice from him. Now he wished he hadn't.

The man had been rolling along on a cart pulled by an old mule, heading out of the hills while McCutcheon headed in. Warily, Mc-Cutcheon had talked to the man, who proved to be cordial and obviously not dangerous. Mc-Cutcheon managed to solicit some directions from the fellow, who told him that he could best reach the Caywood Valley by leaving the wagon road and taking a horse trail he would find a lit-tle farther up. The man had gone on to point out, though, that he couldn't think of any good reason a sane man would want to enter that region just now. Hadn't McCutcheon heard about the killings? "There's the spirit of some old darky fellow who's come back to kill them he hates," the man said. "This here spirit has swore to destroy the Caywoods, and by dang if he ain't off to a good start. It's like that Bell Witch spirit back in Tennessee, what haunted a poor old fellow to death and once sent Old Hickory himself off a-running."

"I'm not aware of any spirit that uses bullets," McCutcheon replied. "Whoever is doing that killing is flesh and blood, I suspect. Anyway, I've got to go there for the sake of an old friend."

"Suit yourself," the man said. "But you'll not see me roaming them woods, especially at night."

Not at all comforted by what he had heard, McCutcheon moved on.

Sure enough, the horse trail had appeared just where the man had said it would. McCutcheon screwed up his courage, said a quick, silent prayer, and left the main road behind.

Now, some hours later, he wished he hadn't. The trail had eventually petered out to nothing, vanishing entirely like a road to nowhere. McCutcheon wondered now if he'd taken the correct trail after all. The day was nearly over, and worst of all, what seemed likely to be a fierce storm was building up overhead.

McCutcheon was lost in a piney forest, shelterless, and about to be drenched and potentially fried alive by lightning. The notion of murdering spirits didn't seem so far-fetched anymore.

He'd encountered no evidence of habitation in this immediate area. He hoped the falling of darkness would reveal some welcoming lamp-light through the woods, a place where a kind native might give shelter to a wandering stranger.

Thunder pealed, then echoed back from some-where in the distant west. McCutcheon felt an electric tingle in the air, the moist wind rising against his face, the sense of a storm about to break.

He had to find shelter soon.

McCutcheon mounted the top of a hill and looked down across a broad, mostly wooded val-ley. To his disappointment, there was no evi-dence of a single soul. Not even a road.

But he was wrong. A closer look revealed a cabin standing in what appeared to be a clearing overgrown with weeds and brush. It was the undergrowth that had hidden the place from ini-tial view.

Clearly this was an abandoned cabin, but under the circumstances that was fine with Mc-Cutcheon. A man didn't have to worry about asking permission to take shelter in a place where nobody lived.

He trotted down the slope toward the cabin as

the thunder pounded again, and a lightning bolt split the sky.

The cabin was indeed abandoned, and partially fallen in on one side. But the roof remained over most of the structure and looked fairly sturdy. He could keep dry, at least.

He found himself a corner and spread out his bedroll. He would spend the night here and worry about finding his way again come morning. He considered building a fire, but the fireplace was at the end of the cabin that had fallen in, inaccessible, and Jim didn't want the bother of searching out stone slabs and kindling to allow him to build a fire directly on the puncheon floor. The night would be cold, but he'd been cold before. He would get by on a meager supper and keep himself warm in his blankets.

The storm struck in earnest while he was still eating. He watched it through a window, and blessed the builder of this place for his skill in roof-making. Even in this dilapidated condition the cabin shed water, on its good end at least. Not a drop fell through in the area in which Jim sat. He leaned back against the wall, eating slowly and marveling at the fearsome splendor of the lightning. In the relative safety and coziness of his shelter, McCutcheon was not disturbed by the storm.

A shattering spear of lightning slashed down from the heavens, rent a tree on a hillside not far

away, and knocked Jim out of his complacency
rather quickly. He actually felt the heat of the
strike, and the thunder blast was like the explosion of an overcharged cannon. McCutcheon
ducked reflexively, holding his breath and covering his head with his hands.

He looked up again quickly, though, when he
heard something unexpected. A gunshot, out in
the woods . . . a rifle, from the sound of it, fired
not more than two hundred yards away from
him.

Two more shots then sounded, one from the
same area as the first, the other from farther
away. McCutcheon heard the sing of a bullet.

If he didn't know better—and he realized he
didn't—he'd think a gunfight was under way.

McCutcheon scrambled to the nearest window
and looked out into the driving rain. Another
shot—and this time he saw the flare of the blast.
A lightning flash followed at once, revealing
something he hadn't noticed before: The abandoned cabin he was in was not the only one
in the vicinity. There was another cabin about
fifty yards away, almost fully hidden by trees
and undergrowth.

The rifle blast he had seen had come from inside that second cabin.

More gunfire came from the forest. This was a
shoot-out!

McCutcheon ducked, wondering what was behind this encounter, who was shooting at whom, and why. And what he should do about it.

Probably nothing. Whatever this affair was, it wasn't his. He need not get involved . . . could not, in fact, without knowing which man was on the right side of this battle.

A bullet thumped into the wall of the cabin that McCutcheon was watching, and the person inside screamed . . .

And suddenly everything was different.

The scream was a woman's.

McCutcheon was amazed and appalled. Whoever was out there in the woods was shooting at a woman! He was so stunned by this that it didn't cross his mind that the woman was doing quite a good job of shooting back.

He couldn't sit by. He had to help that pinned-down woman.

He scrambled back across the room and fetched his rifle. He then went to the cabin door, out into the driving rain. His intention was to make for the cabin where the woman was holed up, and to join his defense to hers. Together they could drive away the gunman in the woods.

McCutcheon reached the edge of the cabin. It was very dark at the moment, but lightning could sear down at any time and reveal him once he left his hiding place. The gunman in the woods might then send a few shots his way.

The woman screamed again, words that Mc-

Cutcheon couldn't make out. Forgetting his
worry, driven by a masculine impulse to protect,
he launched himself out into the rain and headed
for the cabin.

He was halfway across before he realized that
the woman might take a shot at him, too. She
couldn't know who he was, or that his intention
was her protection.

Lightning flared, revealing him. In the moment of inky darkness that followed, he tripped
over a root and fell onto his face.

Gunfire blasted from the woods. Lead sang
above him.

McCutcheon tried to rise, but he slipped in
mud and fell again. He looked toward the woods
as lightning flashed once more.

For less than a moment he saw the form of the
man who had fired at him. The man had
emerged from behind a tree, looking in his direction, rifle half raised.

The lightning, brief as it was, was enough. It
did not require long to recognize so familiar a
figure as that of Jake Penn.

Jake Penn . . . haunting the woods, firing at a
woman . . . and firing at him.

A new flash of electric light illuminated the
sky and the storm-whipped landscape. Penn was
there still, the rifle raised, pointed in Mc-
Cutcheon's direction.

McCutcheon came to his feet. "Jake!" he

shouted. "Jake, don't shoot!" But his shout came in tandem with the thunder, and his words were lost.

Jake Penn's rifle fired, and McCutcheon spasmed and fell with a yelp of pain, grabbing his side.

Chapter Seven

Soaked, dazed, and with his side stinging, McCutcheon struggled to his knees, then to his feet. He looked at the area from which Penn had fired, unable to believe his old friend had shot him. Fortunately, he was fairly certain the bullet merely grazed him.

He didn't hear my shout, McCutcheon thought. *And he didn't know it was me. He wouldn't have shot if he'd known it was me.*

But why would Jake shoot at *anyone* so blatantly? And why would he engage in a gun battle with a woman? This wasn't the Jake whom McCutcheon had known.

McCutcheon lunged toward the cabin where the woman was, grimacing against the pain and the rain that hammered his face.

Another shot rang out, this time fired at the cabin, not at McCutcheon. Whatever was motivating Penn was certainly powerful. He clearly wasn't going to back away from this fight.

McCutcheon reached the side doorway of the

cabin. A rickety door, ajar, hung loosely on one hinge. He shoved against it and rather than open, it fell in with a crash, and McCutcheon staggered in right across the top of it.

A lightning flash showed the woman near a front window, wheeling to meet him, her rifle up.

"No!" McCutcheon yelled. "Don't shoot . . . I'm here to help you!"

"Who are you?" Her voice was equal parts fright and determination. He knew she would kill him if she doubted his good intentions.

"I'm Jim McCutcheon, a stranger to you. But I'm here to help you fight off Jake—to fight off that man out there."

She levered her rifle.

There was only one way to prove himself before she dropped him. He ran to the nearest window in a rush, knelt, and fired a shot blindly into the forest in the sniper's general direction. He was struck by the surrealness of shooting at his former partner, especially given that he didn't even know what this fight was all about.

But his act seemed to melt her doubts about him for the moment. She turned away from him and back to her own window, pumping two bullets from her Henry rifle out into the stormy night.

"Go away!" she screamed into the darkness. "Go back to hell where you belong!"

Penn answered with a shot that sent her ducking. McCutcheon heard the slug slap into the wall at the back of the cabin.

Angry, McCutcheon fired at the area from which the flash of Penn's shot had come, but he couldn't keep himself from pulling the shot to one side. He didn't really want to kill Jake Penn, even though Penn had already shot him.

The storm was beginning to abate, but slowly. The battle, however, ended abruptly. McCutcheon and the woman remained at their two windows, ready to fire, but there was no further gunfire from the woods, no more visible activity, even during the flashes of lightning, which now came further and further apart.

"What if he's coming down this way?" McCutcheon asked the woman. "We have to be ready."

She did not reply. He could barely make out her form in the dark cabin, crouched tensely at the window. She wore trousers like a man, and he could tell nothing of the length of her hair because of the floppy hat on her head. If not for her voice he would not have known she was a woman at all.

No more gunfire sounded. The lightning and thunder moved on far to the west, now just distant grumblings and flashes in the sky. The rain dropped to a much gentler shower, falling straight down now as the wind diminished.

McCutcheon turned at last and found himself facing the woman and her rifle, which was aimed in the general direction of his stomach.

"Drop your rifle," she demanded.

He did.

"Tell me your name again, and why you came here."

"My name is Jim McCutcheon. I came here to help you."

"Why?"

"A man was shooting at you. It ain't right for a man to shoot at a woman."

"You shouted at that man out there like you knew him."

She was right. McCutcheon realized how that must look to her. He couldn't think of any reaction but denial. "No, I didn't. I shouted to him, but he's a stranger to me."

"It sounded to me like you called him by name." Her voice carried clearly the inflections of the Ozark country.

"There was thunder. It fooled your ears." He wished he could sound more convincing.

"I'll shoot you. He tried to kill me . . . he's killed some of my kin already. If you're with him . . ."

"*With* him? He *shot* me! Why would he shoot me if I was with him?"

She had no immediate answer. McCutcheon wished he could see her face, read her expression. But it was too dark. She said, "I don't know why he shot you. But I don't know why he's killed my kin, either."

"You're a Caywood?"

"Yes. But how did you know that?"

"I know that there's someone killing members of the Caywood family, and leaving notes on the bodies, if that's what you mean."

"How do you know?"

"I read it in the newspaper."

"Why are you here?"

McCutcheon realized he could not tell her the truth. He could not risk letting her know that the man murdering her family might be the same man who was so recently his partner. "I'm . . . I'm looking for a man who robbed me back in Fitch. He took my money and several of my possessions while I slept in the hotel." Embellishing a bit, he added, "Stole my horse, too."

"So you came all this way tracking a thief?"

"It was a good bit of money he stole, and not all of it mine. I'd sold some livestock, you see, and had the price of it in cash. And some of the personal items he stole meant a lot to me. My late mother's wedding ring, for instance."

"How'd you get so far off the road?"

McCutcheon could quit lying now. "I got lost. Ashamed to admit it, but I did. When the storm started coming in I came looking for shelter and found that cabin yonder. I didn't even know there was another cabin nearby until I heard the gunfire."

"I swear you called him by his name."

"I don't know his name. I also don't know what I might have said . . . I'm not used to getting shot at. I may have been babbling nonsense for all I know." McCutcheon grimaced and touched his side. "I'm bleeding, and I'm hurting real bad. Will you lower that rifle? I want to see how bad off I am."

She hesitated, but not long. The rifle came down. "You sit down and get your coat and shirt off. I've got matches."

McCutcheon obeyed. The air was cool against his bare skin and made him shiver. He sat down on the floor. "Is it safe to strike a match? He may still be out there."

"Can't let you bleed to death, can we?" She knelt beside him, removing her hat. McCutcheon was aware of her long hair spilling out and across her shoulders. She struck the match.

For the first time, McCutcheon got a good look at her face. He was stunned. Despite her masculine clothing, she was a spectacularly lovely young woman. Her eyes focused on his bleeding wound; she frowned evaluatively. She was too absorbed in studying his wound to look at his face and realize he was staring at her. He glanced down at his wound just before the match burned almost all the way down.

She shook the match out. "The bullet just cut a furrow into your skin. A lot of bleeding, but nothing serious, I think."

"It looks fairly deep to me," McCutcheon said, feeling a little worry all at once.

"Let me take one more look," she said.

She struck another match. He looked in horror at the bleeding furrow in his side, then up at her. He noticed something that shocked him.

"You're bleeding, too," he said. "Your arm . . ."

"I took a bullet," she said calmly. "Nothing serious. Don't worry about it. No need to worry about yourself, either. Your wound isn't bad."

If it wasn't, why did he feel so faint? McCutcheon remembered with chagrin that his mother had always said women were far better than men in dealing with wounds to themselves.

McCutcheon wouldn't let this lovely young lady be more resilient than he. "Let me bandage your arm," he said. "We've got to stop the bleeding."

She rose and walked away from him. "'*We've*' not got to stop anything. I can bandage it myself."

He arched his brows. A stubborn and self-reliant woman, this one. He didn't mind having his offer rejected, though. His side was beginning to hurt pretty seriously, and he still feared he'd pass out. He wished the bleeding would stop.

"How did you happen to be out in such a remote area at this kind of hour and in this kind of weather?" he asked, trying to sound stronger than he felt. He heard cloth tearing. She was tearing a strip for bandaging from the tail of the man's shirt she wore.

"Not really your business, but I was hunting," she said.

"What were you hunting?"

"A killer."

"You actually came looking for—" He caught himself just in time to avoid saying Penn's name. "For that man out there?"

She was busily bandaging her arm now. "He's killed my kin. Distant cousins and such up mostly. The latest, though, was my uncle, Tom Caywood. A close uncle, almost as close as my own father. His son, my cousin Ben, found him. He literally fell over him in the dark while he was running from the murderer himself."

"Did Ben survive?"

"Yes. He made it home. But finding his father like that changed him. He's angry, full of bitterness, like dynamite about to explode. If he goes after the killer himself he'll probably get himself killed. He's too out of control. So I came to kill the murderer myself."

"I can't believe somebody like you would do such a thing."

He felt her glaring at him through the darkness. "What's that supposed to mean, 'somebody like me'?"

"Just that . . . it's not usual, you know, for manhunting to be done by a pretty, young woman such as yourself."

"Well, I did a pretty good job of it, I'd say! I found the bastard, didn't I? I'd probably have killed him by now if you hadn't come nosing in!"

Now McCutcheon began to feel riled—which was a good thing, because he suddenly didn't feel quite so faint anymore. "Seems to me I helped you out considerably. Once the odds became two to one, he backed off. If I hadn't helped you, you'd be dead by now. And keep in mind that I didn't *have* to help you at all. I could have laid low and let him kill you, and nobody but God above would ever have been the wiser."

"You give yourself a lot of credit, mister. This isn't your matter, anyway."

McCutcheon thought wryly how it might be more his matter than she could know. "I take it seriously when I see another person about to be murdered."

"He'd not have murdered me. I'd have killed him."

"There's no point in arguing over it now. The fact is we're still in here, both of us are hurt, and he's still out there. He may not have left for good, you know. Should we stay here?"

"We stay until morning. We at least have the

protection of these walls. And its too wet for him to burn us out."

Her reasoning made sense. "All right," Mc-Cutcheon said. "We'll stay until morning. And then I'll take you back to your home."

"What makes you think I need your help? You think I'm afraid to go back without your protection?"

McCutcheon began to realize how deeply into his mouth he was inserting his own foot. She took offense at everything he said. "Maybe it's me who feels the need of protection by you," he said. "Who's to say he might not think I'm a Caywood and kill me, too? If you'd let me travel with you to your home come morning, I'd be obliged," he said.

She sighed slowly. "All right. You can come with me. But for now, shut up. If that man comes around again, I'll never be able to hear him with your jaws flapping so."

"I'll say no more. Except I will ask you your name."

"Susanna."

"Susanna Caywood. It's a pretty name."

"Will you never be quiet? Just sit over there and keep your ears open, and maybe we can make it out of here alive come morning. How's your wound, by the way?"

"I think the bleeding is about stopped."

"Good. Then keep your eyes peeled and your

ears open. We can't assume everything is okay until morning comes."

"You're sure a bossy woman, you know?"

"I sure am. And maybe if you'll listen to me and shut your trap, we can manage to stay alive the rest of the night."

She returned to the window and reloaded her rifle while staring out into the darkness. The storm had emptied the sky of moisture and the clouds were fading. As time passed, the darkness outside became a little less thick; McCutcheon eventually could make out her profile in the window. The line of her profile was classically beautiful. Given her mode of dress and her residency here in these western backwoods, he wondered if she had any inkling of just how lovely she really was.

McCutcheon greeted the morning light wearily, having not slept at all the night before. The light revealed his beautiful companion looking closely at him, openly evaluating him and not seeming at all shy about it. He had the disconcerting feeling that the evaluation wasn't yielding results he would find flattering.

"Well, we've made it through the night," McCutcheon said, grinning. She didn't smile back, which made him feel foolish.

She said, "If we're going, now is the time."

"Guess so. Do you have a horse?"

"I had one. When I got shot I fell off it. It ran away."

"Then I guess we're walking, huh?"

She didn't reply, and again he felt foolish. Was she trying to make him feel that way? What kind of woman was this? She was an intimidating one, hard to admit though that was. And tough as a boot to be sure.

He glanced at her arm. The blood from her wound was dried now, rusty colored. She had done a decent job of bandaging it, under the circumstances. She moved as if it caused her no pain at all. McCutcheon's own wound hurt like the devil, making him groan and grunt with every motion, even though he tried not to. It wasn't bleeding anymore, but he did believe the wound was worse than Susanna had presented during the night. If the shot had hit him at a different angle, he probably would have been killed. He might have pointed it out, but knew she would just disdain him for it.

"How far to where you live?" he asked.

"Seven miles. Give or take a mile or two."

"I've got some food in my pack over in the other cabin. I'm glad to share it."

"Good of you," she said. "But I ain't hungry."

McCutcheon collected his meager possessions, and the two of them set off. They kept mostly silent while they traveled. McCutcheon had decided that if she wasn't going to eat, then it

would be perdition's coldest day before he'd eat,
either. He'd not be outdone by a female.

But after a couple of miles he decided that
kind of thinking was foolish. Susanna Caywood
made him feel like he was in some sort of compe-
tition, the winner to be determined by who could
be the most stoic and self-denying, but the devil
with that. He was hungry, so much that the intensity of it actually took his mind off the throbbing bullet furrow in his side.

He dug into his pack and ate a couple of cold
biscuits, doing his best to make them seem as en-
joyable as possible. He'd give her one, but only if
she asked.

She never did. The miles fell away behind
them, until at length they reached a road and
began following it. It wound out of the woods
and into an area of cleared fields. McCutcheon
saw barns, stables, and cabins spreading across a
wide valley.

"Is this the Caywood Valley?"

"It is."

"Your family owns all this land?"

"My family settled this whole region years
ago. They wrested everything we have out of
barren wilderness. It was all ours . . . until the
Harpers came along."

"I've heard it said there's bad blood between
the Caywoods and the Harpers."

She didn't answer him right away. He wondered if he'd overstepped a line. Then at length she said, "There are a lot of foolish things in this world."

McCutcheon stopped, his attention captured by something he'd just seen. "Looks like we've got visitors on the way."

Chapter Eight

She'd already seen them. "Not visitors," she said. "That's my father and Uncle Luke coming."

"Which one is your father?"

"The one in the lead. The tall one with the gray hair and the beard."

Another rider, previously hidden by the others, became visible. "There's a third one, too," McCutcheon said.

"That's Ben, my cousin. The one whose father was killed."

McCutcheon noticed they were armed and riding toward them with sufficient haste to worry him.

"Susanna, they don't know who I am. Any chance they might assume the worst and—"

She anticipated where he was leading. "Don't worry. Just let me talk to them. I'll explain who you are."

He nodded, though he didn't like the notion of being protected by a woman. He had more male pride than he had realized—and Susanna Caywood had a way of challenging it in everything she did. Again he wondered if she was doing it deliberately.

"What's your father's name?" he asked.

"Macnamara Caywood. Everybody calls him Mack."

"Mack Caywood? The family patriarch?"

She frowned at him a little suspiciously. "Just how much do you know about us, anyway?"

"Only what I read in the newspaper and heard back in Fitch."

The trio of riders thundered up. Mack Caywood, a quite distinguished-looking man in his early sixties, held a Greener shotgun with sawed-off barrels. Mack gave an initial impression of strength, but a second look revealed an underlying appearance of illness. His eyes, though piercing, were surrounded by vague dark circles, and his shoulders had that slight, permanent stoop that comes of perpetual coughing. The two other riders carried Winchester rifles. All three men wore Peacemakers on their hips.

"Susanna, are you all right?" Mack Caywood demanded.

"Yes, Pap. I'm fine."

"The hell you are! You were gone all night, and your arm is bloodied!"

"I was shot, Pap."

The man came out of his saddle with the litheness of a much younger man, but he was instantly seized with a fit of coughing so severe that it stopped him cold. He almost dropped the Greener. Susanna went to his side.

"Who shot you?" he choked out between coughs, looking harshly at McCutcheon. "Was it this bastard?"

"No, Pap. It was *him*. The killer."

"Dear God, girl!" Mack coughed some more before he could finish. "What made you ever go out there?"

"I went looking for him, Pap. I wanted to find him and kill him and put an end to all this."

Mack Caywood could only gape at his offspring.

"Damnation, girl!" exclaimed Luke Caywood, who was still in his saddle. "What the devil are you trying to do? Get yourself killed?"

Susanna ignored her uncle, keeping her eyes on her father and her chin up high in pride. Despite himself, McCutcheon found himself giving her a mental cheer. Though he agreed with Luke's assessment, he couldn't help but admire Susanna's determination and self-confidence.

Ben Caywood said nothing, but looked at his cousin admiringly, obviously proud of her.

Mack coughed a bit more, then got hold of himself and stood up straight. "Susanna, I ought to put you over my knee like you were still a child. Hell, I ought to haul you over to Hulltown and have Jake Flatt lock you up in the jail for your own safekeeping!"

"I think you did the right thing, Susanna," Ben Caywood said.

Mack wheeled and shook a finger at the young man. "You shut that yap, Ben! Stay out of this!" He turned to Susanna again, who looked back at him in a way that managed to combine respect with defiant self-assurance. "Susanna, we've had to all but hog-tie Ben to keep him from doing the very thing you did, and you don't help nothing by doing it yourself. Lord, girl! I never thought I'd raised a fool!"

"I did what I thought was right, Pap. We sat back doing nothing when those he killed were just distant cousins and such, and because of that, now Uncle Tom is murdered, and Ben is without a father."

"Don't lecture me about the death of my own brother, girl!"

"Somebody's got to stop him, Pap. And better I should try than Ben. He's too wrought up about his father to do a proper job of it. And I knew that if I went looking, and that murderer saw me, he would think I was an easy kill, being just a woman. I'd get a better chance at him than any of you."

"You did a foolish and dangerous thing, Susanna. Do you not know you had us all in terror all night, worrying about you? Mercy, girl, I'm

nigh glad your mother has gone on to glory so
she didn't have to be here to suffer through the
kind of worry you put us through this past
night!"

"I didn't plan for things to happen like they
did, Pap. I didn't plan for him to shoot at me. I
was going to shoot at *him*."

"Which only goes to show how ill-prepared
you were for such a thing! It ain't your *place* to
do such things, girl!"

"It's not my place to stand by, either, and not
respond when someone kills my kin. I loved
Uncle Tom, Pap. Just like I love Uncle Luke, and
Ben, and you. When somebody hurts one of you,
they've hurt me, too."

Mack's face was red, but the color was fading
in evidence of declining anger. He coughed a little more, then turned his attention to his daughter's bloodied arm.

"How bad is your wound, honey?"

"Not bad. It just nicked me." She gestured toward McCutcheon. "My friend here was shot,
too."

My *friend*. McCutcheon gratefully took note of
the word.

Mack looked coldly at McCutcheon. "Just who
is this 'friend'?"

"His name is Jim McCutcheon. He helped me.
If not for him, I might not have survived."

McCutcheon barely managed to hide his astonishment. She had seemed so disinclined to give him any kind of credit before that he'd been concerned she wouldn't do so now, when it really counted. He'd certainly not had any anticipation of her crediting him with saving her life.

Susanna glanced at him; their eyes met for a second and he hoped she could read in his the appreciation he felt.

Ben Caywood eyed McCutcheon. "He has the look of a Harper about him."

"He's *not* a Harper," Susanna said forcefully. "You see the Harpers in every stranger's face, Ben."

Mack was examining her bandaged arm. "We need to get John Mark to take a look at this."

"It's not bad, Pap. The bullet went right through, like a tunnel. Up close to the skin."

"I want to know the whole story." His gray eyes swept McCutcheon. "And I want to know a little about this here hombre, too. Mr. McCutcheon, you'll be coming with us."

It was not a request, but McCutcheon treated it as one. "I'll be glad to, Mr. Caywood."

Part II

Dark Valley

Chapter Nine

McCutcheon expected an immediate and intense grilling by Mack Caywood, but it didn't happen that way.

After being taken to the Caywood house, he spent most of the next hour seated in a straight-backed chair in the front parlor. He was alone there, but young Ben Caywood remained in the next room, near the door, the entire time McCutcheon was there.

McCutcheon knew he was being guarded, however subtly. Meanwhile, Susanna was elsewhere in the house, talking to her father. He could hear Mack Caywood's coughing fairly frequently; it sounded quite bad, not like a normal cough.

McCutcheon wondered with a little trepidation just what Susanna was telling him.

With nothing else to do, he studied the large room he was in. This house, two stories and made of logs, was bigger and more nicely furnished than he had anticipated. This might be the backwoods, but this was no woodland hovel by a long stretch. Mack Caywood was clearly a man of significant means. Based on what Susanna had said, the family's land holdings alone would be enough to give them stature.

McCutcheon heard motion in the next room, then a girl's voice: "Where is he, Ben?"

"He's in there," Ben replied, his voice so quiet that McCutcheon could barely hear. He sounded sullen, and McCutcheon wondered why. "But you stay out of there. Your father is talking to your sister about everything right now."

McCutcheon thus learned that Susanna had at least one sister. From her voice he judged her to be a younger one. He wondered if she was as pretty as Susanna.

"Is he mad at her?"

"Wouldn't you be? The dang fool girl went hunting for that murdering darky! And dang if she didn't find him and get shot, too." Ben paused. "She shouldn't have done it. It should have been me who done it. Maybe it will be, next time."

"She wasn't shot bad, was she?" This time the girl sounded worried.

"No. John Mark already fixed her up with a bandage, and says it will heal up good."

Instantly the girl's voice sounded light and energetic again. "Is that stranger-man in yonder handsome?"

"How would I know what's handsome and what ain't? I ain't no girl to notice such things! Lord, Deborah! What a fool you are!"

My, my, thought McCutcheon, *what a snapping tone!* Grief, anger, or both were clearly weighing heavily on Ben Caywood.

"I'm no fool, and Susanna ain't, either. We're just brave and bold and know what we want." She paused, then added with a telling emphasis, "At least Susanna went and tried to do something about all the bad things that have happened. She didn't just sit home moping about it."

McCutcheon sat up straighter, definitely paying attention now. This Deborah seemed to actually be baiting her cousin.

Ben's response was restrained, but the restraint sounded forced. "Deborah, your sister went looking for a killer. That's foolish. Foolish for a girl to do, anyway."

"You'd do it. You wouldn't think that was foolish."

"I'm a man. There's a difference."

"You ain't a man. You're still a boy. I reckon that me and Susanna got as much right as anybody to go looking for killers or doing anything else we want to do. Maybe I'll go looking for that killer myself! I ain't scared, and it's sure more than *you've* done!"

Ben's voice became icily serious. "Don't talk that way. And don't you try to say that I'm some kind of coward. When my pa went missing I went out looking for him even though I knew the killer was out there. And I came nigh to being killed myself. I was chased by that murdering bastard, Deborah! Right after I fell across my own father's corpse! So don't talk high and mighty with me just because you think it's really fine that your sister took a fool's chance. I know how dangerous that man is. Don't go into those woods. You don't leave these grounds. It's too dangerous."

"It's always been dangerous, with the Harpers around. You can't let that make you into a coward. I'll not let myself be a prisoner in this house."

McCutcheon grinned. Even as an outsider to this family he could tell what was going on: This young lady was toying with her cousin, saying things just to set him off. And he seemed to not even notice he was being played like a piano.

"You could get yourself *killed*, girl! Just like Susanna almost did."

"You're just jealous because Susanna proved she's braver than you, and her a *woman*."

McCutcheon winced. This young woman knew how to strike a male in a way that hurt. Mack Caywood should put this girl in charge of castrating his livestock; she had some obvious talents in that direction.

"Shut up, Deborah! Just shut up! Go up to

your room, or outside, go anyplace! But don't you talk to me that way again! And don't you leave these grounds unless you want to wind up filling the next hole in the graveyard."

"I ain't leaving this room until I get a look at that fellow in there, I don't care how mad you get! I want to see if he's handsome."

McCutcheon didn't know whether he was handsome—he believed he was, but a man could never be sure about himself—but one thing he knew: He wasn't deaf. Did these people always talk about visitors as if they were senseless pieces of furniture?

"You stay away from that door, Deborah!" Ben commanded. "Get away from here, now, before I go fetch Mack!"

She didn't go away, at least not instantly. McCutcheon saw her face, very briefly, bobbing out from the edge of the doorjamb, her big eyes taking him in. She was indeed as pretty as her sister, very much her image, in fact, but younger.

She smiled brightly at him and was gone in a moment.

"He *is* handsome!" McCutcheon heard her whisper to her cousin, but loudly enough to make sure McCutcheon could hear her. "You should have told me how fine he looks, Ben!"

"Get out of here!" Ben bellowed at her.

McCutcheon heard her laugh as she departed, and shook his head. Absolutely cruel! What was

it with the women in this family? Susanna had
made him feel like a weakling almost from the
moment he'd met her, and young Deborah had
just emasculated her cousin for the sheer fun of
it—never mind that he was freshly bereaved and
grieving.

He wondered what kind of woman their late
mother had been. Strong-willed and forceful,
probably.

Strong-willed women . . . Emily was one, in her
own way. Emily and her constant correction of
his grammar, straightening of his collar, reproval
of his behavior whenever he was doltish. Once
they were married, Emily would be queen of the
household, no question about it.

Odd how hard it was to think of being married. Especially now, away from Texas. He'd
hardly thought of Emily since he'd left. This real-
ization unsettled him.

He sat, frowning at the wall across from him
as he gently touched his wounded side, which
was beginning to hurt worse than ever.

Mack Caywood appeared in the door, shaking
McCutcheon out of his reverie. He looked
solemn but not threatening. He coughed, his
shoulders heaving, but managed to keep it under
control with an effort of will so great Mc-
Cutcheon could see it.

"Mr. McCutcheon, might I interest you in a
cigar?"

"Of course. Thank you."

"Then come on back here. I've got sort of an office room. Kind of a messy place, but I like it. Come on. Don't you be concerned about my cough, by the way. It isn't consumption. Nothing catching. I've visited some fine doctors in some big cities and had that verified. If I were a threat to the health of my family, I wouldn't continue to live among them." He paused. "Mr. McCutcheon, just to make our introductions official, my name is Mack Caywood. I'm Susanna's father. None of that, I suppose, is news to you."

"Yes, sir, I mean, no, sir. I'm Jim McCutcheon, from Texas. Pleased to know you." The two men shook hands.

The room was as messy as promised, and cluttered as well. McCutcheon found a chair, scooted some papers and books out of it, and sat down. Caywood made his way to a desk, cleared himself a corner, and sat down right on the desktop. He picked up a cigar box, plucked out one for himself, and handed the box to McCutcheon.

McCutcheon fired up his cigar. Caywood didn't light his. "I can't smoke these things anymore, sorry to say," he said. "The old lungs, you know. I'm down to chewing my cigars. Not very satisfying. I suppose I should just give them up completely." He evaluated McCutcheon while his unlighted cigar did a slow roll from one side of his mouth to the other. "You know, sir, I didn't know what to make of you when you showed up with my daughter. Especially with her wounded like she is."

"I hope her wound isn't serious. She said it wasn't."

"It'll be all right. She'll feel it for some weeks, but she'll never let on. That's her way. Stubborn and never letting it show when she hurts. Her mother, God rest her, was the same. Susanna's been that way since she was a little thing. Very willful."

"I kind of gathered that, sir, just from the brief time I've been around Susanna."

"You were wounded yourself."

"Nothing much. It just plowed me on the side. But it bloodied my shirt some, as you can see."

"We'll provide you another shirt."

Mack coughed violently and abruptly, his face reddening. With another effort of will he brought it under control. He glanced down at the cigar and tossed it over into the fireplace. "Can't even enjoy them unlighted anymore because of that blasted coughing. Sometimes it's even hard to sit down and eat because of it." He eyed McCutcheon. "You seem to be in some pain."

McCutcheon hadn't realized it showed. Indeed he was hurting; his wound sent a steady dull throb through him, and he felt rather sick. After Susanna's display of toughness, though, he wasn't about to complain. "I'm handling it. Mostly I'm tired. Last night was a long one."

"Yes. And about that . . . I want to thank you for helping Susanna. She is a headstrong and foolish female. No notion of danger, no fear at all. How many young women would go in search of a murderer all alone in a wilderness like this one?"

"Not many." McCutcheon paused. "But your younger one, Deborah . . . I think she might."

"What do you know of Deborah?"

"She stuck her head through the door while I was in the parlor. Curious about me, I think. Mostly I overheard her talking to Ben in the next room. She seemed to think the idea of a young woman chasing a murderer all by herself made good sense. But I think she was mostly having a bit of fun getting her cousin stirred up."

Mack slowly shook his head. "I fear for Deborah. Less common sense about her even than her sisters. And she does have that tendency to toy with people, men especially." He coughed and made a faint grunt that told McCutcheon the cough hurt.

"You said 'sisters.' So you've got more than two daughters?"

"There's Marie. The middle child. The most sensible of the three in some ways. But way too much of a worrier. As nervous as a trapped mouse. She frets her life away hour by hour."

"Do you have sons as well?"

"No sons. But Ben and his little brother, Jeremy—my brother Tom's boys—have been like sons to me. Now, I suppose, they are my sons, since their real father is dead. Tom was the most recent victim of whatever murderer is out there. Poor Ben found him, in the darkness. Fell across his body. And he almost became a victim himself. He ran through the woods with the killer on his heels. How he managed to get away, I truly don't know."

"Who do you believe this killer is, Mr. Caywood?"

"Call me Mack. I have no idea who it is. All I know is that he's a black man, and that he leaves notes on those he kills that attribute his actions to vengeance for some woman named Nora. I don't know who Nora is, or was, or have any concept about who this murderer can be. It's very frustrating, and it makes a man suspicious of all that's around him, and every stranger. If not for the fact that your skin is white, and that this killer was still out there shooting at Susanna while you were with her, you would be in very serious trouble."

"I'm not the killer, sir. I promise you that."

"Oh, I know that. But there's somebody out there who is, and I fear for what will become of us all if we don't stop him very soon."

"What made Susanna decide to go after the killer alone?" McCutcheon asked.

"The girl has always believed she can do anything. But it was grief that made her do it. And anger. And pity for Ben. And frustration and fear that lack of action would only get more people killed. Who can say? The girl left home once when she was ten, looking for a strayed cat. She went twenty miles into the woods and spent a night alone, without any of us knowing where she was. Her mother thought she was dead for sure. Then she came back—with the cat."

McCutcheon grinned and puffed his cigar. "Quite a woman."

"Quite a *girl*. I can't think of her as a woman, though I know she is. To me she'll always be my little girl. That's the way it is with fathers, I think. Especially those who have lost their wives and have only their daughters to provide the female presence in the household." For a moment or two Mack lowered his head and was deep in thought. Then he looked up at McCutcheon.

"You had your horse stolen from you back at Fitch, Susanna tells me, and came following the thief into our region here?"

"Uh . . . yes."

"Among other things, I raise livestock. I've got plenty of good horses. In thanks for you helping Susanna, I want to give you one to replace the one taken from you. Not on loan and not through sale. A gift."

"Give me a horse? I . . . I can't do that, Mack. I don't have grounds for accepting such a generous gift."

"Of course you do. I want you to, and God knows you've earned it. Susanna says you saved her life."

McCutcheon didn't know what to say. "I . . . thank you, sir. Mack. And call me Jim."

Mack stood; McCutcheon did the same. Mack stuck out his hand. "You can't know the depth of my appreciation, Jim. And I'm sorry for the way you were first received. You have to understand the set of my mind at that time . . . we have been afraid of the worst."

"I understand."

"There's been so much loss here lately, you see. All these murders. And this killer . . . it's like he's not human. He can come and go, appear and vanish. Some believe he's not human at all. But I'm not a superstitious man. Our killer is flesh and blood, not some disembodied spirit."

McCutcheon was thinking about the woodsman's skills of Jake Penn. Penn could be almost ghostlike in the wilderness.

"There has to be some powerful reason for anyone to murder so many in cold blood."

"Murder in cold blood has a long history in

these parts, I'm sorry to say. Have you heard of the Harper family?"

"Heard mention of them, yes."

"You know of the feud?"

"Not much. I know it's existed, but I don't know what it's about."

Mack grinned sadly. "There's the rub. It all goes back so far that not many do remember. It was a simple land dispute to begin with. That matter is long forgotten. Now the feud goes on of its own accord. Anger and bitterness and vengeance for old wrongs on both sides. The original reasons don't even matter once you reach that point. The feud is foolishness. Pure foolishness. With effort, and a lot of compromising and turning the other cheek, I've been able to cool this ridiculous fight to the point that there's been very little to it but a lot of posturing and name-calling. Enough time, enough further effort, and I might actually be able to end the thing altogether. But now that's all falling apart. These murders are poisoning everything."

"Do you believe the Harpers may be behind the murders?"

"I've considered the possibility. Ben believes it, and so does Luke, sometimes. But there's a new twist now that makes that notion seem like nonsense to me. A couple of Harpers have turned up dead, too."

"That would seem to rule them out for sure."

"Indeed. But Luke and Ben still won't let go of the notion that the Harpers are somehow behind it."

"Do you have a theory yourself?"

"It was Caywoods the killer went after first. It could be that there was some old Caywood offense that sparked this. Or, it could have its origins in something that both the Harpers and the Caywoods did. Something that's been forgotten, or that maybe was never known by most to begin with."

McCutcheon fearfully obeyed an impulse. "Have you ever heard of a man named Jake Penn?"

Mack shook his head. "No. Can't say I have. Who is he?"

"It's . . . just the name of the man who may have stolen my horse. I heard somebody call that name back in town."

"Wish I could help you, but I don't know him. Let's go take a look at some horseflesh. Let's select you a good one. You got no saddle, I assume."

"Not here I don't."

"Well, that poses a problem." Mack scratched his whiskers, thinking. "Tell you what: There's two, three old saddles at the tack house. With a little work, one of them could be made usable for you. But it'll take some time. You'd have to stay at least until tomorrow."

This was not an unwelcome prospect. But McCutcheon couldn't respond too eagerly. After all, he was supposedly hot on the trail of a horse thief and shouldn't be willing to let that trail go cold by hanging around this place.

Fate intervened at just the right moment to give him the pretext he needed to accept Mack's invitation.

"Jim," Mack declared, looking down, "you're bleeding."

McCutcheon looked down. Sure enough, blood was soaking through his shirt. The furrow that Penn's bullet had cut through his side had opened anew and was spilling a significant amount of blood. McCutcheon himself was shocked. He'd obviously broken the scabs through movement.

"I think I might need some help," McCutcheon said, suddenly light-headed.

"Tell you what, my friend, you're going nowhere today," Mack said. "We'll get that bandaged. There's an old black fellow here name of John Mark who is as good as any book-learned doc I've ever seen. He's already patched up Susanna. We'll get him to do the same for you."

Chapter Ten

John Mark couldn't have been a day under seventy-five, and was maybe older than that. But his hands were steady and he examined McCutcheon's wound with the clear eye of an expert. He anointed the furrow with a salve that, astonishingly, pulled out almost all the pain and also helped staunch the bleeding. He topped it off with a well-prepared bandage.

"That'll heal up good for you, sir," the old man said. "You just don't go twisting and moving around a lot for a couple of days and you ought not have no more trouble."

"Thank you, John Mark."

"You're welcome, sir. You going to be spending the night here, sir?"

"I am. And forget the 'sir.' Call me Jim."

"If you don't mind it, sir, I'd just as soon do what I feel the best with."

"All right." It made McCutcheon a little sad. He and Penn had talked a lot of times about old black folk that both had known, ones who became so accustomed to being deferential and subservient that they could behave in no other way. John Mark was apparently one of these.

"It's a good thing you're staying, sir. It ain't safe to go out in these woods no more."

"The murders, you mean?"

"Yes, sir."

"Surely I don't need to worry. I'm neither a Harper nor a Caywood."

"I'd think you'd already be worried, sir, in that he done shot you."

"Good point. But I was helping out a Caywood at the time."

"He may not forget you done that, sir."

"It was dark. He probably couldn't see me enough to know who I was. Who do you think the killer is, John Mark?"

"I wouldn't know, sir. The devil himself, I figure. It's the purest wickedness that's going on here, sure as the world. The devil is in these woods. The very devil."

"But the devil was an angel once, they say."

"Yes, sir, that's the truth. But why do you say that?"

"Just wondering if it's possible that a man who was at one time a good man could become capable of such wickedness, if he was pushed hard enough."

John Mark squinted, thinking hard. "No, sir, I don't think so. Not *that* degree of wickedness.

Any who could do so much bad as that would have to be pure wicked from the beginning."

McCutcheon stared into a corner. "If that's correct, then it can't really be Jake out there," he muttered.

"What was that, sir?"

"Oh . . . nothing. Just thinking out loud. Talking to myself."

"Yes, sir. I do that myself sometimes, just thinking out loud. Now, sir, I suggest you go lie down somewhere and let that wound get started healing again. Meantime, sir, I'll get started to working on fixing up that saddle Mr. Mack is giving you. He done told me all about that, and the horse, too."

"Mack is a generous man."

"He is, sir. He's a fine man. As long as you don't cross him, or hurt his kin. That's why I actually pity this devil in the woods. Mr. Mack may be a kind and generous man now, sir, but when he finally gets his hand on that killer, God help the man. God help him."

For McCutcheon, supper at the Caywood table was a surreal affair.

Ben Caywood sat at one corner of the long table, glowering and deep in his brooding grief. He gave occasional glances to McCutcheon, his expression unreadable.

Susanna, her arm neatly bandaged, seemed

calm and controlled, her eyes clear and her gaze steady. Deborah Caywood was full of energy, showing no signs of being affected by the bereavement this household had suffered; she spent much of her time glancing at McCutcheon with open interest. Luke Caywood was silent, deep in thoughts that he kept hidden. He, too, seemed to find McCutcheon of interest, but there was no judging what conclusions he might be drawing. His eyes were somewhat bloodshot; McCutcheon suspected he'd been drinking in the afternoon.

Marie Caywood, the raven-haired sister who was between Deborah and Susanna in age, seemed sad and burdened; she hardly looked at McCutcheon, or anyone else, at all. Jeremy Caywood, Ben's younger brother, seemed nervous and afraid.

At the table with the family was John Mark. McCutcheon was pleased by this. Many such families would not have let a servant, particularly a black one, share their table. But John Mark was treated as one of them. McCutcheon's respect for the family increased.

The food, prepared by the daughters, was common fare, but excellently cooked. McCutcheon ate ravenously, self-conscious because of Deborah's flirtatious stares.

He listened to the supper table conversation and was intrigued by the way Mack kept it steered away from the subject of the murders and the Harpers. Clearly Mack's belief was that such matters were not for the table. But McCutcheon knew those same matters surely dominated all other hours. A heavy burden indeed, and weighing heavier on Mack's shoulders probably than on any other.

McCutcheon's bed was in an upper room, hardly more than an oversized closet. The quarters were cramped, but he slept deeply, and all his questions and fears for a time went away.

When he awoke the next morning, he was refreshed, though his wounded side inflicted a continuing dull ache upon him. The bandaging had held, though, and no blood had seeped through.

The first rays of the morning sun were working their way through the slats of his shuttered window. Rising, he crossed the little room and opened the shutter, looking out.

He'd not seen the property from this point of view until now, and now noticed for the first time a small building, made of logs, standing a quarter mile away. A cross mounted on the peak of its roof let him know this was a church. Beside it was a graveyard.

In the graveyard a man was standing, hat in hand, looking down at a grave. McCutcheon could just make out that it was Ben Caywood.

McCutcheon pitied the young man. What

must it be like to find the murdered body of your own father? No wonder he brooded and grieved and seemed so marked by what he had endured.

McCutcheon dressed, washed in the cold water in the basin that had been provided for him, and slipped downstairs. The smell of breakfast wafted enticingly from the kitchen. The Caywood daughters were up and at work; he could hear their muffled chatter and the clanking of pots and pans. It was a pleasant noise, especially combined with the aroma of cooking bacon and the scent of coffee.

For the moment, though, McCutcheon wanted most of all a chance to stretch his legs and get some fresh air. The air had a different quality here in these mountains than it did in the Texas flatlands to which he'd recently become accustomed, and he found it invigorating.

McCutcheon left the house. In the yard he met John Mark carrying tools toward a shed, hard at work despite the early hour and his advanced years.

"Good morning, Mr. McCutcheon."

"Morning, John Mark. How are you today?"

"Quite fine, sir. But worried."

"How so?"

"I sense there's to be trouble very soon, sir. It's a feeling I get, where I can tell when something's going to happen."

"Trouble of what sort?"

"I fear to say, sir. I fear to say."

McCutcheon wasn't superstitious, didn't believe much in premonition and so on, but John Mark had a quiet authority that gave his words weight.

"These feelings of yours, do they often prove accurate?"

"Most always, sir."

"Then maybe you should warn the family."

"I'll do that, sir. And I'll warn you, too. Them hills are full of danger today. I think he's watching."

"That's a mighty lot to know just from a feeling, John Mark."

"I know, sir. But most times, when I know these things, I really do know."

"Whatever trouble comes, I believe Mack, at least, will face it fearlessly."

"Oh, yes, sir. I've been with Mr. Mack now more years than I can count, and I've never seen him back down from anything in fear, nor from doing anything he made his mind up about. And his brother Mr. Luke is more stubborn yet."

"I don't know much about Luke. How does he make his living?"

"He helps his brother. Mr. Luke's got his own little house over on the other side of that strand of pines you can see on the ridge. Mr. Mack is the one who owns most of the stock, most of the land, and so on. Mr. Luke has got a bit of property to call his own, but it's Mr. Mack who is really the big boss around here."

"What kind of man is Luke?"

John Mark hesitated. "He ain't the man his brother is, I can tell you that."

"What do you mean?"

"Mr. Luke is fond of the bottle. If not for Mr. Mack looking out for him, making sure he stays straight, I don't know if Mr. Luke would still be among the living. He'd have drunk himself into his grave. Don't say I said that, please, sir."

"I'll not say a word. Has Luke ever been married?"

"At one time. She thought better of it, and went her own way."

"I'm supposed to be married myself, and in just about a month."

"Do tell! Congratulations to you, sir."

"She lives in Texas, a little town called Sweetbush. Her name is Emily."

"Best wishes to you both, Mr. McCutcheon."

"You know, John Mack, if I were not a man already engaged, and if I lived closer about these parts, I think the lovely ladies here in this household would be quite an attraction to me."

"They're lovely, no question about it. But there's hardly ever a man who comes calling."

"That's hard to imagine."

"It's the feud, sir. People have heard such tales that they stay away. It's too bad. Mr. Mack is a good-hearted man. He likes people. He'd open his house to the whole world if he could."

"It was my understanding the feud hasn't been a real fighting feud for some time."

"A feud is a feud, that's how I see it. That's how others see it, too. There's history here, history of men killing each other, hating each other, fearing each other. People are afraid it could all break out like it used to be, back when it was more than the sky getting shot at by the Harpers and Caywoods. Back in those days men from the two families roamed these woods looking for each other like men hunting snakes."

"You seem a smart man, John Mark. Who do you think is behind these killings?"

"I truly have no notion, sir."

"No knowledge of any Nora out of the past, somebody maybe the Caywoods and Harpers hurt? Somebody caught in a crossfire, perhaps . . . something like that."

"I can't say, sir. I've known of folks by the name of Nora before. But I know nothing about any Nora that would have somebody getting revenge on the Caywoods."

McCutcheon decided to take a chance. "John Mark, have you ever heard of the name Penn?"

"Penn . . . I don't believe so, sir. Why do you ask?"

"It was a name I heard called back in town, that's all. It doesn't mean anything."

"I wish I could tell you something, sir." John Mark was looking now at Ben Caywood over in the graveyard.

McCutcheon, noticing, said, "That young man is overburdened with his grieving."

"Yes, sir. But it's his anger that's the danger to him, and to everybody else. He's headstrong and reckless."

"Like his cousin Susanna."

"Yes, sir."

"Think I'll go talk to him."

"That would be a good thing, sir. That boy needs sense talked to him right now."

Chapter Eleven

McCutcheon's intent, though, was not so much to talk to Ben as much as to let Ben talk to him. Ben had come close to the killer. Maybe something had been said or done that would give a clue about what was behind all this and could help McCutcheon ascertain whether the culprit really was Jake Penn.

Ben saw McCutcheon coming, and greeted him only with a silent stare.

McCutcheon nodded at him and glanced down at the fresh grave, marked with a wooden cross on which the name TOM LEROY CAYWOOD was crudely carved.

"Good morning, Ben."

Just a grunt in reply.

"I'm mighty sorry about your father."

"So am I."

"My own parents are dead. It was hard to lose them. But it would be harder yet to find your own father murdered."

Ben stared at him. "Why are you here?"

"I just came to speak to you, and express my sympathies."

"No. I mean, why are you *here*, in this valley?"

"My horse was stolen. I tracked the thief and he led me here."

"Where were you going before the horse was stolen?"

"You know, those kinds of questions are usually not the kind folks ask of strangers. It's considered downright impolite, most places I've been."

"Them I'm downright impolite. I'm also a man who has lost his father to a murderer without a face or a name, and I'm wary of strangers."

Ben had called himself a "man," but Mc-Cutcheon had his doubts about that. Ben Caywood seemed still a boy to him. "You never saw the killer up close, I suppose."

"No. It was dark. I knew he was behind me, chasing me. He was close, but I never saw him. Only two or three have ever seen him and that was from a distance. Why are you so interested?"

"He shot me, remember? A man shoots me, I want to know who he is, and why."

"He shot you because you were trying to help Susanna. That's not hard to figure out."

"Maybe. Or maybe he's taken to shooting at

anybody he sees. I'm told that some Harpers are dead, too. So it's not just your family he's after now."

Ben made a contemptuous-sounding grunt at the mention of the Harpers. "I don't know that any Harpers are dead. That's nothing but rumor."

"Why would they make something like that up?"

"The Harpers hate the Caywoods. Our families have feuded for years. It's the Harpers who are behind all these murders. That murderer is under their hire."

"Then what's all the business about Nora and vengeance and so on?"

"A bunch of made-up nonsense. Something to throw us off and make us think it's not the Harpers responsible for the killing. But it *is* the Harpers—I'm sure it is. Think how easy it would be to hire somebody to go killing off members of the family you're feuding with! Maybe they've hired themselves a black man who don't mind killing. Maybe he's one of the Harpers themselves done up with paint on his face."

"But it can't be the Harpers who have hired the killer. Some of the Harpers have been killed by the same man."

"How do you know? There's Harpers all through these hills. It would be easy to make a couple of false graves and claim the killer has struck at your own family, too. Just to throw everybody else off the scent, you know. It would be just like the Harpers to do something like that."

"No disrespect to your line of thinking, Ben, but that seems kind of unlikely to me. Claiming somebody in your family is dead when they ain't means that person has got to lay low from then on so as never to be seen. That's a mighty clumsy scheme."

"Maybe the ones they claim are dead really *are* dead, but they died from some natural reason. Or maybe they're just made-up names stuck on empty graves. Nobody knows all the Harpers. They're everywhere. Like rats and bedbugs. Make a false grave and slap the name Whatever-the-hell Harper on it, and who's to say there never was such a man?"

It seemed to McCutcheon that Ben was ready to accept the most unlikely explanations as long as they confirmed his prejudices. "You seem bound and determined to make the Harpers out as guilty at any cost."

"You seem bound and determined to defend them."

"I don't defend them. I don't even know them."

"So you say."

McCutcheon ignored the obvious implication. "You truly hate that family, I gather."

"Hate ain't strong enough a word, Mr. Mc-Cutcheon. They ain't made a word strong enough to tell how I feel about the Harper family. Especially now that my father is murdered."

"I don't get a sense of such strong hatred from your uncle Mack. He tells me he's tried to halt the feud."

"Mack's a good man, but with the kind of goodness that can blind a man to the truth of the way things are. Uncle Luke knows better. He tried to make peace with some Harpers many years ago, and it went bad for him. He knows now that you can't trust those snakes. He hates the Harpers nearly as much as I do."

A bell clanged over near the house.

"Breakfast is ready," Ben said. "You'd best get to it."

"You ain't eating?"

"I had a cold biscuit when I got up. That's enough for me. I ain't got much appetite since my father was murdered."

"Well, I've got a big one, so that's a bell I'll answer."

"Do that. And maybe sometime later, when you're all healed up, you and me can go hunting Harpers together. What would you think of that?"

"Are you serious?"

"Why would you think I wouldn't be?" Ben smiled, and it was unsettling.

Without saying anything more, McCutcheon turned and walked toward the house.

Chapter Twelve

There was no doubt about it: The Caywood sisters were blessed with the rare kind of beauty that actually was enhanced rather than diminished by the stark light of morning streaming through the windows. McCutcheon enjoyed the company as much as the food, though Deborah made him a little uncomfortable with her open flirting. Her father, who had returned from the stables for his breakfast, gave her occasional reproving looks that went fully ignored.

Marie bustled about, somber and laden with sadness and worry, removing empty dishes and refilling coffee cups. Susanna maintained her usual rock-solid, confident persona. Her very posture bespoke an utter inner confidence.

Studying Susanna surreptitiously, McCutcheon decided that an earlier perception of her as a firebrand like her cousin Ben was not completely accurate. She and Ben had a similar purposefulness of manner and attitude, and no doubt a similar stubbornness, but Susanna's personality was tempered somewhat by greater maturity. Ben came across as someone with no restraints beyond the natural limits of his own passions and impulses. If he, rather than Susanna, had gone out hunting the murderer, there would probably be one more dead Caywood ready to be laid in the family plot.

Luke Caywood was not present for breakfast. Luke had eaten supper here the night before, but he apparently had returned to his own house after McCutcheon retired.

Little Jeremy sat hunched up and silent at one corner of the table. He glanced at McCutcheon from time to time but never spoke.

"What are your plans now, Jim?" Mack asked McCutcheon.

A good question. McCutcheon had come to find whether the woodland killer was Jake Penn, but had no clear idea now how he was going to proceed. "I'll move on, I suppose," McCutcheon said, unable to think of anything else to put forth. These folks weren't running a hotel, after all. "I do appreciate the hospitality you have shown me."

"Oh, you can't go yet," Mack said. "John Mark told me your wound is still prone to open. He recommends you take some bed rest to let those stitches do their work and let the healing set in . . . and believe me, you can take John Mark's advice with the same assurance as if it came from a physician. I insist you stay at least a day or two more and let that wound knit."

"That's kind, but I can't impose on you good people forever."

"A day or two more ain't imposing. There's also the very important fact that John Mark ain't finished fixing that saddle for you yet. Unless you want to walk or ride bareback, you've got no option but to keep on being our guest." He turned his head and coughed, a deep, rattling, ugly kind of cough.

"Well . . . I guess I'll stay, then."

"Good."

"Maybe there's a way I can make myself useful. Some kind of chore or work."

"I told you what John Mark said. The only task you have before you is taking a rest. We don't want you busting open on us."

"Good Lord, Pap, do you have to talk about such things at the table!" Marie exclaimed. It was the first time McCutcheon had heard her speak a word.

"Oh, don't be so squeamish, girl!" Mack chuckled.

Marie glared at him, eyes moistening. She burst into tears and left the table. She stood at the mantel, crying, her back to her family.

Susanna and Deborah glanced at each other. Deborah rolled her eyes.

Mack shook his head and stood. His look

made McCutcheon suspect that this kind of scene had been played out many times through the years in the history of the Caywood family.

"Marie, what's wrong?" Mack asked.

Marie just kept crying. Mack went to her and led her back to the table. "Sit down, Marie. You're all worked up. Drink some water and calm down."

Marie suddenly blubbered, "All the death . . . poor Uncle Tom! Poor Uncle Tom! What's going to become of us? He'll kill us all, like he killed Uncle Tom! I just know he will!"

"Quiet down, Marie. Calm yourself."

"I can't . . . I can't . . . I just want it all to stop!"

This time Susanna rolled her eyes and impatiently murmured, "Merciful heaven!"

Marie heard this and went from blubbering grief to fierce anger. She aimed a trembling finger at her sister. "Don't sit there judging me, Susanna! You think yourself so big and brave because you went chasing a killer! Well, I think you're a fool for doing it, a fool who only made it worse for us all! He'll hate us all the worse because of what you did! He may come kill us all in our sleep! I can't bear it anymore! I can't!"

"Oh, you goose, do you really think what I did made anything worse? How could it be worse than it already was?" Susanna replied.

"Hush, both of you!" Mack commanded. Then, to Marie: "Daughter, I want you to go to your room, lie down, and stay there until you feel better. How long since you've slept a night through?"

"A long time . . . I'm so afraid!"

"I'll take her up to her room and get her tucked in," Susanna said.

"I can go myself!" Marie bellowed. "Do you think yourself so important that no one in this family can do a thing without you, Susanna Caywood?" Marie stomped out of the room.

Mack went through another coughing spell; then, when it was over, he shook his head. "Sorry you had to witness that little outburst, Jim. This family is in a state of disruption right now."

"Understandable. How could it be otherwise? You folks are holding up better than most would, I'd say." McCutcheon took a final bite and stood, lifting his dishes. "I'll carry these in for washing."

"I think Marie is being absurd," Susanna said. "I'll not tremble for fear of anyone!"

"Me, either," Deborah said. "And Marie's so weak-stomached, too! Can you believe she got so worked up just because Pa said that about Mr. McCutcheon? I wouldn't faint or anything even if Mr. McCutcheon's wound did break open!"

"That's a good thing," McCutcheon said as he suddenly set down his dishes and collapsed back into his chair. Fresh blood was soaking through his shirt. "Because I think it just happened."

"Jeremy," Mack said, rising and heading toward McCutcheon, "go fetch John Mark, right now."

Ten minutes later, John Mark was leaning back from his examination of McCutcheon's wound and shaking his head sadly. "Yes, sir, Mr. McCutcheon, but I do believe we're going to have to stitch on you some. I'd hoped that furrow would close on its own, but it ain't doing it. Unless we stitch you, that thing will reopen again and again and putrefy on you."

McCutcheon, supine on his bed with his bandage removed, stared at the ceiling and forced himself not to react to this bad news. The reason for his stoicism was the presence of Susanna, who had come in with John Mark to help with the examination of the wound. As much as McCutcheon hated the thought of John Mark taking a needle and thread to him, he'd be hanged before he'd show any visible dread in front of Susanna. She would only hold it in contempt.

"Let's get on with it," McCutcheon said nonchalantly. "I'm tired of feeling like a cracked china doll."

"I think you should purify the wound first, John Mark," Susanna suggested.

"Yes'm," John Mark replied. "I believe I
should."

"Purify? What do mean, purify?" McCutcheon
asked.

"It might hurt a little," Susanna said. "But it
also might save you from infection."

"I'm going to pour a bit of whiskey in it, sir,"
John Mark said. "It'll burn like the devil. If you
yell ain't nobody going to think the worse of you
for it."

Susanna smiled at him.

Just the thought of alcohol in that bullet furrow was almost enough to make him scream, but
there was no way McCutcheon would let himself
do that. They could pour hot brimstone in his
wound and he'd not react. John Mark could say
what he liked, but McCutcheon knew that Susanna would indeed think the worse of him if he
howled. Her smile gave him the notion she was
secretly looking forward to hearing him do it.

"Maybe we should purify Susanna's wounded
arm at the same time," he suggested.

"I did that myself when John Mark first bandaged me," she said.

"She didn't even flinch, sir," John Mark said.
"Women are strong like that. They can take pain
better than a man. The Lord made them that way
for childbearing, you know."

McCutcheon gave her a quick, cold grin.
"Glory hallelujah."

Susanna's smile had not faded. "I'll go get the liquor, John Mark." She left the room.

"I apologize to you for not having thunk to purify your wound before now," John Mark said.

"Don't worry about it," McCutcheon replied. "If you had, I'd probably just be sitting around right now all bored and restless, instead of having all this fun."

Susanna returned with the bottle in hand.

"Do you want to do it, or shall I?" she asked John Mark.

"You go right ahead, Miss Susanna," John Mark said.

Susanna approached and pulled the cork from the bottle. "If you want to yell, just do it."

He laughed. "Yell? I won't yell."

She positioned the bottle above the wound, and tilted it.

McCutcheon would be informed later that the scream he let out could be heard all the way over at the stables.

After the whiskey burn came the ordeal of being stitched. Though John Mark did the job expertly, it was an agony for McCutcheon, who was drained of energy when it was done. He wanted nothing more than to escape into sleep again.

He did sleep, soundly at first, but then increasingly troubled by disturbing dreams. He envisioned himself being tortured in various ways.

All the while someone stood by laughing. It sounded like Susanna.

He awoke sometime in the afternoon, thinking about Susanna and wondering why she brought out such a competitive spirit in him. Around her he felt compelled to prove his masculinity and toughness, because she seemed to be so much stronger than he was. She was strong, brave, stoic, and yet wonderfully feminine at the same time. A flower of iron, but still a flower.

He noticed how much he was thinking about her, and how little he was thinking about Emily.

Masculine voices rose from elsewhere in the house. Someone was arguing.

He recognized Mack's as one of the voices, and realized the argument was going on in the room directly below him, the same office room in which he and Mack had had their first talk.

"No!" Mack was declaring. "We'll do no such thing! We have no grounds at all to believe the Harpers are to blame, and I'm damned if I'm going to gather up some fool vigilante army and go running off to restart an old war that, thank God, we'd finally begun to see fading away! Blast it all, Luke! I can see Ben thinking such foolishness, young and impetuous as he is, but you're supposed to be a grown man, with a bit of intelligence about you!"

"It has to be the Harpers doing this, Mack. Who else would have cause?"

"There've been at least two Harpers killed, Luke! You're telling me they've hired some black man to go killing off Caywoods and had him murder a couple of their own kin just to make it look less suspicious?"

Luke presented the same response that Ben had given to McCutcheon, alleging that the Harper deaths had been in some way faked. Then he went on, "Why the hell do you defend the Harpers, Mack? Have you got so determined to end this feud that you're willing to turn your back on the fight that this family has fought since before me and you were even born?"

"What have we gained from that feud, Luke? How has it helped us? Why would you want it to go on?"

McCutcheon pushed himself up a little in the bed, turning his head so he could hear better. The effort made the stitches in his side pinch and pull, and he winced. But the stitches held. John Mark had done a good job.

"Like it or not, that feud is part of who we are, Mack. The Caywoods and the Harpers were meant to fight each other. It's been going on since Caywoods long before us were fighting the redskins and each other back in Kentucky, and it's our duty to keep up what they begun."

"Dear Lord, brother . . . you really believe it's our family duty to keep on making the same mistakes our fathers and grandfathers did, forever, just as a family tradition?"

"It's called heritage, Mack. Something apparently you don't understand."

"Oh, I understand heritage. Heritage is like a river or a stream. When there's good pure water in it, that's fine. But when you fill that stream full of poison, then it becomes dangerous. And as long as our heritage is that feud, then our heritage is a poisoned river. And it's our duty to change it and make it clean and good, not just to keep the same old poison flowing."

"Listen to you! You sound like a preacher!"

"Better than sounding like a fool!"

"Mack, reason this thing out. There's somebody out there killing off Caywoods. Who has a history of hurting and killing our people? The Harpers. Now, unless you're ready to believe that somebody besides the Harpers has come up with some whole other reason to hate and murder Caywoods, it seems sensible to me that the obvious suspects are the Harpers. All this Nora nonsense, notes on bodies and such, and these tales of Harpers being murdered, too—it's all distractions or lies, trying to throw us off the right track."

There was a long pause before Mack replied. "You know what scares me the most about this, Luke? That you have actually managed to persuade yourself that such nonsense could really be true. Do you really believe the Harpers are smart enough to come up with a conspiracy and fake deaths and all that?"

Luke's tone was as cold as January. "Maybe it's you who is believing nonsense, brother. Leave it up to you, and we'll just sit by while our people are killed off one by one. As far as I'm concerned, it's time to quit sitting by. It's time to respond."

A door slammed. McCutcheon heard it open again at once, and Mack's voice yell, "Luke! Come back here! We're not through talking yet! Come back here!"

McCutcheon moved carefully, mindful of his stitches, and pulled back the corner of the curtain covering the only window in his little room. He saw Luke Caywood striding purposefully across the yard, toward the stables, ignoring his brother's calls for him to return.

McCutcheon let the curtain fall and lay back down again. He felt deeply troubled. Pressures were building in this tragedy-stricken household. It couldn't be long before something exploded.

He wondered if he would be caught in that explosion. And maybe Jake Penn as well.

Chapter Thirteen

Luke Caywood closed his eyes as he drank from the upturned bottle. His moistened lips pursed shut as he savored the taste of the whiskey a few moments before swallowing. Swiping his mouth with the back of his hand, he considered whether to take another swallow. He was drinking too much, he knew—but it was so good, so satisfying, and he was so angry just now. And when Luke Caywood was angry, he drank. Even more than when he wasn't angry.

He turned up the bottle again, swigged, then corked the bottle and set the whiskey aside. His brain felt deliciously fuzzy. But he worried about getting too drunk out here in his own house, which was out of view of Mack's big log dwelling. Though so far all the deaths had happened in the hills, out in the woods, there was no way to know the pattern wouldn't change. The killer could slip into this little outlying house, with a knife in his hand, and if Luke was passed out drunk it would be easy to . . .

Luke shut off the thought with a shudder. Ironically, the image in his mind was so disturbing that it led him to uncork the bottle again. Just one more swallow, then he'd stop.

He was stoppering the bottle again while swishing the whiskey around in his mouth, when he glanced out the nearest window. What he saw made him choke on the liquor.

There was a movement in the woods . . . Somebody slipping through a grove of trees, moving in a surreptitious manner. For a moment Luke had a relatively clear glimpse of the man—average height, strongly built . . . a black man.

Luke began to tremble; the bottle almost fell from his hands. Numbly, he set it on the nearest table and feared his knees would buckle beneath him.

His rifle . . . where was it? Then he remembered: He'd left it at Mack's house the day before, for John Mark to clean.

His shotgun, then. It would have to do. In fact, it would be better, because its pattern was wide. Even if fired by a shaking drunk it would have some chance of striking its target.

He went to the cabinet, opened it, and removed his shotgun. He loaded it hurriedly, then went to the window again, looking for the watcher in the forest.

No sign of him now. But that meant little. This murderer had the ability to vanish like smoke.

More than one search had been made for him, only to uncover no traces at all. From this ability to vanish had been born the rumor—easier to believe than Luke wanted to admit—that the killer might not be human, but literally an avenging phantom.

Luke lingered by the window, shotgun in hand, his breath coming in hard and ragged gasps. Occasionally he glanced toward that tempting whiskey bottle. But he forced himself to resist it. Had to stay on his toes, ready to react. His life might depend on it.

Perched at the window, keeping somewhat to one side so as to not be readily visible from outside, he studied the grove of trees and eventually decided that the man was gone. This brought little relief, because it meant he now had no idea where the lurker was. He might be slipping around the house, planning an ambush, or readying to set the place afire.

Luke heard a noise . . . someone moving behind the house. He wheeled, so panicked he almost fired the shotgun blindly into the inner parts of his own dwelling. Holding his breath, he crept through the house toward the opposite door.

Someone was out there, at the door . . .

Luke leveled the shotgun. He would shoot right through the doorway, taking no chances. He felt sudden exhilaration mixing with his fear.

He was about to single-handedly bring to an end the threat to the Caywood family! He imagined the shock of the Harpers when they realized that their hired murdered had himself been slain.

"Take *this*, damn your soul!" he whispered, centering his aim right at the middle of the door.

His finger was already tightening on the trigger when he heard Ben's voice: "Luke? Are you in there?"

Luke lowered the shotgun and shuddered violently. He'd almost killed his own nephew. He laid the shotgun on the floor and staggered weakly to the door, throwing it open.

"Luke! You look like you're sick!"

Luke reached out and pulled Ben inside, then pulled the door closed and slumped to the floor.

"Luke, what's wrong?"

"I almost . . . God forgive me, boy. I thought that you were . . ." He could hardly catch his breath. "He's out there, Ben. That murdering darky . . . I seen him in the woods, watching the house. When I heard you, I thought . . ."

Ben pulled his pistol from its holster, quickly checked to make sure it was fully loaded, then headed out the door.

"No, Ben! Wait! Don't you go out there!"

But Ben pressed on, circling the house toward the woods, keeping as much cover as possible between himself and the grove.

Luke knew he should go after Ben, either to

stop him or to help him look for the murderer. He felt deeply ashamed of himself . . . but it was not enough to spur him to action. What could he do, anyway? He was too liquored up to be anything but an added danger.

He listened, fearing the roar of a gun at any moment, but heard nothing. After a minute he pulled himself together enough to get to his feet and make it into the next room, where he uncorked the bottle and took a long, deep drink.

When Ben returned to the house a few minutes later, Luke was deeply relieved.

"If he was there, he's gone now," Ben said. "Are you sure you saw him?"

"He was there. I know he was. Black face, looking back at me from that grove of trees."

Ben nodded. Luke saw that he was shaking.

"That's a brave thing you did, going out there to look. But I shouldn't have let you do it."

"I had to do it, Luke. Otherwise . . ." He didn't seem to want to continue.

"What?"

"Hell, Luke, it's what Susanna did! It gnaws at me! She went out looking for that devil in the woods, and I've done nothing to compare . . . even though I'm a man, and it was my own father, not hers, who got killed! It should be me who went out hunting that killer, not her!"

"You *did* go looking, Ben. You looked just now.

And you were out looking the night you found poor Tom."

"I was looking for my father that night. But Susanna was actually looking for the killer himself. It was pure courage. Far more courage than I've yet shown. At first I was proud of her—I told her so. Then, the more I thought about it—"

"What Susanna did might have been brave, but it was foolish, too," Luke said. "She shouldn't have done it."

"It's time we *all* got foolish. My father was killed, Luke! Your own brother, and Mack's— and yet here we are, pretty much doing nothing but sitting around and waiting for somebody else to die, while Mack goes on about how he don't believe it's the Harpers doing this and how the feud has to be ended and such bilge and rubbish as that. And now the damned Harpers are getting so bold they're sending their hired killers right up to your very doorstep. We've got to do something more than what's being done. Mack is too soft and won't see the truth. And the sheriff is a Harper man, so there's no help for us from the law."

"So what can be done?"

"We got to go to the source of our problems, and create some problems in turn."

"What do you mean?"

"It's time to quit hunting the killer, and start hunting Harpers instead. Until they get a taste of their own medicine, this thing ain't ever going to end. This is a war, Luke. It's time we started fighting it that way."

Ben's words were almost enough to knock Luke sober again. "Don't be talking about something that'll get you killed, boy."

"It won't get me killed if enough of us stick together and do what needs doing. We'll never get Mack involved, but maybe there's enough others about who would do it. There's Caywoods all over, Luke. We can go out and round up a whole army of Caywoods. We can take these hills back from the Harpers."

Luke rubbed his chin nervously, saying nothing.

"Luke, I know you think the same way I do. I heard you and Mack arguing earlier, back at the house. It's what made me decide to come on out here and talk to you."

"What do you propose we do?" Luke asked.

"Bring the Caywood clan together. Get us all to working as one group, fighting the common enemy. The family has gotten too spread out over the years, like a bunch of different families instead of one. We need to change that if we don't want the Harpers to overrun us. They're making a mockery of us with their hired killer. They think we'll never figure it's them behind it. They're sitting back and laughing, thinking we can't touch them. But if all the Caywoods work together . . ."

Luke nodded and completed the thought for his nephew. "Then we can hit them where it counts. We can end this feud by winning it. All right. Makes sense to me. I'll go along with it."

Ben smiled. "Good. We'll start with just you and me riding out together to start talking to other Caywoods. We'll start with Michael Caywood . . . he's got influence with the farther-out branches of the family. We'll recruit him to help us. We'll get the stone rolling. Before we're done, it will be an avalanche, and the Harpers and their killer will be the ones crushed under it."

"All right," Luke said, beginning to feel excited at the prospect of actually doing something about what was happening. "You and me together."

"You'll have to lay off the liquor while we do this, Luke. You realize that, don't you?"

"Yes. I'll do it."

"Come back to the house with me. It ain't safe for you to be out here alone. We'll not tell Mack about our plans."

"Mack may not let me in the house after the go-round we had before."

"He'll let you in. He's a forgiving man. Too forgiving, really. That's his problem."

*   *   *

From the forest, the watcher observed the two Caywoods as they left the house. He was utterly silent and had been here for a long time, even while the younger Caywood had been looking around in the grove for him. He was a skilled woodsman, generally capable of not being seen when it suited him. He only regretted that his skills had failed him somewhat a little earlier, when he had recklessly allowed himself to be seen from the house. He'd spotted the elder Caywood at the window and known he had been observed.

He vowed to be even more careful from now on. The next time, no one would see him, until he was ready for them to.

He waited until the Caywoods were out of sight before he moved. In moments he was deep into the forest.

Chapter Fourteen

Jim McCutcheon wasn't accustomed to excessive bed rest, and it didn't take him long to reach his limit. At first—apart from overhearing the disturbing argument between Mack and Luke Caywood—he had found it pleasant to lie in bed in the afternoon. Certainly it was just what his wounded side needed. But soon enough, lying abed simply made him feel like he was sick. Which, ironically, made him feel tired, which only kept him in bed.

He had actually dozed off into a half slumber when he became aware of someone at the door. He sat up, then pulled the covers up higher over his body. His visitor was Susanna.

She smiled, rather surprising him. "I'm sorry if I'm intruding. I just wanted to come see how you were getting along."

"I'm fine, thanks. John Mark did a good job of stitching me up. How's your arm?"

She moved her bandaged arm, which was at

the moment propped up in a sling. "Doing well. It does hurt a little."

"Good. I mean . . . good that it's doing well. Not the hurting."

She cocked her head and looked closely at him. "I think I'm making you uncomfortable."

"Well, no . . . it's just . . . uh, yeah, maybe you are, a little."

"Not 'proper,' huh? Is that it? Me being a young woman, you a young man, and here I am in your sleeping quarters."

"I ain't . . . I mean, I'm not sure that your father would favor it."

She laughed. "He probably wouldn't. But I don't always worry about what my father thinks. If I did I would be letting him live my life for me, wouldn't I? Which isn't really the point of living, I don't think—letting somebody else live for you. I tend to do what I think I should and not worry about the rest."

"I figured that out when I found you having a gunfight with a murderer."

She laughed again. It was a remarkable laugh, quite appealing. It showed a side of Susanna that McCutcheon hadn't yet seen, because up until now she'd been of a fairly serious, almost severe, humor. He saw a resemblance to Deborah that was more than physical.

He was about to comment on it, but she spoke

first. "Why did you do what you did a few moments ago?"

"What?"

"Correct yourself from saying 'ain't.'"

He grinned across the top of his quilt. "I'm used to being corrected on my speech, that's all. Now I've taken to doing it myself . . . which I guess is what she's hoping would happen, come to think of it."

"She?"

"My wife-to-be."

A short pause. He thought her smile flickered down a moment. "Oh. I see."

"Her name is Emily. She lives in Texas."

"I didn't know you were to be married."

"Well, there's no reason you should have known, if you think about it."

"What kind of woman is she?"

"A good one. She was . . . she was married once before. And has a son. A fine little boy named Martin Pike."

"Her husband died?"

"No. It was a divorce."

"I see."

"You didn't react too much to that information. Some people find it shocking that I'm to marry a divorced woman."

"There are some divorces, I'm sure, that are justified."

"Hers was."

"When is the wedding?"

"Just a few weeks."

"Congratulations."

"Thank you."

"What do you do for a living, Jim Mc-Cutcheon?"

"At the moment, I'm a merchant. Emily's father has a store in Sweetbush and is about to open up another one over in Whitefield. Emily and I are to operate that second one."

"I wish you the best. Both of you."

"I appreciate it." He smiled at her. "And what about you? I suppose that there's bound to be men interested in a household full of pretty young ladies."

Her smile was sad. "Marie is too nervous and flighty to get much attention from men. But Deborah has a young man, over in Hulltown. His name is Joe Tifton. Pa doesn't like him, though he's a fine young man. Ben and Luke don't like him, either, because he has some friends among the Harper family, and so they don't trust him. Deborah cares deeply for him. She once sneaked all the way to Hulltown to see him, because Pa won't let him come to call on her here. But I think sometimes he does, on the sneak. That kind of thing makes Pa furious."

"What about you?"

She shrugged. "I understand why she wants to

see him. I can't really favor her running off unsupervised, though."

"No . . . I mean, what about you and menfolk? None of my business, I realize . . ."

"Indeed it's not. But you've told me about yourself, so I'll tell you about me. I've got no suitors. I never have, not really."

"I'm surprised, as pretty as you are. I hope you don't mind me saying such a thing."

"You probably shouldn't be, with a woman waiting to marry you back in Texas. You're a spoken-for man."

"I don't think you like me much."

"Why do you say that?"

"Just the way you've talked around me, especially at the start. I felt like you resented me being there."

"I gave you credit for saving my life. A pretty generous gesture on my part, I think."

"It was. But all in all you've seemed to have a harsh tone with me."

She looked away. "Being gracious is not always my strong point."

"Nobody's perfect, they say. I ain't. I mean, I'm not."

"Why does your fiancée correct your grammar?"

"She believes it's important for a man to speak properly if he's going to be in business."

"Most people I've known don't talk any more properly than you do, in business or not."

"I've made the same point to her many times."

"But she won't be persuaded?"

"She's a bit like I perceive you to be in that regard. Not easily swayed."

She tried not to smile but couldn't help it. "Am I that easy to characterize?"

"Let's just say it doesn't take long to realize you are a forceful woman. Out there in that cabin in the rain, I felt like I was a soldier fighting a war with you as my commanding officer."

"It was right for me to direct matters. It was my fight."

"Because you're a Caywood?"

"That's right."

"Your father and your uncle had an argument today . . ."

"I heard it, too. Luke believes the Harpers are behind the murders."

"What do you think?"

"Who can say? It seems unlikely . . . but anything could be true at this point."

A strong impulse struck McCutcheon unexpectedly. He wanted to tell her about Jake Penn, and Penn's quest for Nora, and how the killer in the woods almost certainly had to be Jake. But he faltered, unsure how she would react.

And what if he was wrong about it all? He'd seen the killer in a flash of lightning, and though he certainly had appeared to be Jake, it was always possible it wasn't . . . though how likely was it that there would be another black man who not only looked a lot like Jake Penn, but also had a history related to a woman named Nora?

Susanna looked out the window.

"Two riders are coming in," she said. "It's Luke and Ben, I think. I didn't know they'd gone off together. I wonder if something's happened."

McCutcheon, using the covers to hide himself, scooted to the far side of the bed and wriggled into his trousers.

He joined her at the window and watched the pair ride in. Then his line of vision happened to shift toward the west.

"Hey, is that . . . ?"

"What?"

He was eying a thicket at the edge of the yard. "Nothing," he said after a pause.

He was all at once very aware of standing there beside her, wearing only his trousers. He glanced at her and caught her eye as she glanced back. The moment became uncomfortable.

"I'll go down and see if Luke and Ben are hungry," she said hurriedly, turning and leaving the room without looking at him again.

Chapter Fifteen

McCutcheon joined the family for supper that night. The bed rest had done him much good. His wound was healing quickly, the flesh already binding together again and the stitches beginning to grow uncomfortable.

More uncomfortable yet was the environment of the Caywood household this evening. Luke, clearly under the effects of alcohol, was a blotchy-faced, unpleasant soul, and Ben was keyed up and intense, talking more than usual. When he told the incident involving the black man Luke had seen in the woods, Mack grew very concerned.

"So now he's watching our houses!" he declared. "Not content to murder us in the woods anymore—he's beginning to haunt our very doorsteps!"

"It's the Harpers, Uncle Mack," said Ben, reasserting his familiar theme. "You know it down in your heart as much as the rest of us do. Until we deal with the Harpers we're never going to stop the killing."

"You'd deal with killing by inflicting more of it? No, Ben. No. That road leads to the graveyard and nowhere else."

"If it's full of dead Harpers, then glory be and pass me the bullets!"

The conversation turned into an argument and the argument turned into shouting, spreading around the table, wrapping itself all around Mc-Cutcheon, who kept silent, staring at the peas on his plate. The terrain covered in this family battle steadily expanded while he listened. Before long Ben was admitting before all what he'd said only to a few so far: that Susanna's solo expedition to find the killer made him feel outdone, and that he was determined to not sit back any longer while women did what he perceived as a man's duty. His restraint fading away, Ben ended up insulting Mack's own courage, implying that it was out of cowardice that he was unwilling to launch a full-scale war against the Harpers.

Luke got into the argument as well, mostly just spluttering and cussing and making little sense, until at last he could bear no more of it and backhanded his glass off the table to shatter on the puncheon floor. He got up and stormed away—heading for the nearest bottle, Mc-Cutcheon supposed. Marie soon followed, weeping, unable to stand all the intensity. Little Jeremy, the nearly silent boy whom McCutcheon was beginning to perceive as being quietly eaten away by pure fear, sat and subtly swayed back and forth, blocking it all out, looking like a child version of an asylum candidate.

Somehow the conflict even managed to drag in the matter of Deborah Caywood's beau from Hulltown, against whom Mack railed rather nonsensically. By this point, McCutcheon was getting lost in all this, not sure anymore why this argument was taking place at all. He was witnessing the human equivalent of an uncontrolled explosion. This bereaved and beleaguered family was coming apart before the eyes of a virtual stranger, and McCutcheon caught himself thinking that if the killings were being orchestrated by the Harpers, like Ben said, then the Harpers were certainly achieving their desired end. The Caywoods were being shattered as a family. The killer was destroying even those whom he had yet to touch physically.

When McCutcheon glanced over and saw tears in Susanna's eyes, he knew at that moment that it was time to leave. Even Susanna, the bold and granite-hearted, was beginning to break down.

This was not his place. He'd been here long enough. In terms of his wounded condition it was a little early for him to be traveling, but his stitches were holding up and his flesh was starting to heal. John Mark would have that saddle ready for him come morning. Then Jim Mc-Cutcheon would say his thanks and be on his way.

McCutcheon finished his meal, folded his napkin, and left the table. As he climbed the stairs back up toward his room, the argument around the table continued full-steam.

He met Luke coming back down the stairs, doing a poor job of hiding a bottle he'd obviously sneaked out of some upstairs hiding place. McCutcheon pretended not to see it.

"You'll be staying here tonight, I hope, considering that your house is being watched," McCutcheon said to him.

"I'll be here. Though it's like being in hell as far as I'm concerned."

"These are hard times for your family. I'm very sorry to see it."

Luke muttered something McCutcheon couldn't quite make out and shoved on past him and down the stairs.

The hours already spent in bed, combined with the coffee he'd consumed at supper, stole sleep from Jim McCutcheon.

The argument among the Caywoods had finally subsided, leaving the house quiet and the suffering family members heading for their various beds. In Luke's case, bed was a sofa in a little spare room near the back of the house, adjacent to Mack's office and partially under the one where McCutcheon was. McCutcheon could hear Luke's muffled snores from below.

McCutcheon lay still, listening to the ticking of a clock elsewhere in the house. It seemed to be going dreadfully slow.

Tomorrow he would leave and go . . . home?

No. He couldn't go back yet. He had to know whether it was Jake Penn who had put that bullet wound in his side. And if so, why?

But he wasn't sure how to proceed from here.

The world beyond the walls seemed very dark and threatening. McCutcheon marveled that Susanna had been brave enough to actually venture out alone on such a night as this, actually *seeking* the murderer.

What a bold, brash, foolhardy woman!

But what an incomparable woman, too! Funny how he couldn't stop thinking about her. It frightened him, though, that she was managing to push Emily further and further from his mind.

A noise outside . . .

McCutcheon sat up, listening, wondering why that faint, stray sound outside had caught his ear. Most likely it was merely a dog or a cat, even the wind . . . yet some instinct told him differently.

McCutcheon slipped out of bed and went to the window. Pulling aside the curtain, he squinted out into the darkness, trying hard to see.

He sucked in a sharp breath when he caught sight of the form of a man, hard to see but undeniably there, moving toward the woodshed in the yard, moving like he was trying not to make much noise.

Earlier in the day, when he and Susanna had been looking out this same window while Luke and Ben rode in, McCutcheon had thought he caught a glimpse of a moving but mostly hidden figure out in a thicket at the edge of the yard. He'd quickly persuaded himself that he was mistaken.

Maybe he hadn't been after all. He certainly wasn't now: There was a man out there.

Chapter Sixteen

McCutcheon was about to raise an alarm, but stopped. What if that was *Jake* out there? The Caywoods might gun him down.

Of course, if Jake had turned murderer, didn't he deserve to be gunned down? McCutcheon's conscience told him yes . . . but hang it all, Jake was still Jake! McCutcheon wouldn't stand by and see him killed, whether he deserved it or not. Besides, if Jake had turned bad, McCutcheon wasn't going to let him die without knowing what prompted it.

So McCutcheon kept quiet, got up, slipped on his clothing as quietly as he could, armed himself, and headed down and out into the night.

He was as concerned about not attracting the notice of the person outside as he was about not awakening the household. McCutcheon moved in the darkest areas, creeping toward the woodshed . . .

Back at the house, a door opened. Mc-Cutcheon darted for the nearest bush and crouched there, readying to fire if the lurker at the woodshed made any move to harm whoever was emerging. The only trouble was, McCutcheon couldn't see the lurker just now . . . but the lurker might be able to see him, or see the person who had just left the house . . .

It was Deborah. McCutcheon saw her dart into the yard, a shawl pulled around her shoulders.

She headed straight for the woodshed.

McCutcheon came out of hiding just as he saw the lurker reappear. In the man's hand was a rifle, though not upraised. Deborah saw the man and stopped, then turned and let out a yell, muffled by her hand, as she saw McCutcheon appear.

"Deborah!" McCutcheon yelled as loudly as he could. "Run! Get back to the house!"

McCutcheon raised his gun and aimed at the dark figure near the woodshed. The man was so startled he dropped his rifle, then stumbled backward away from McCutcheon.

A light came up in the house. Mack's voice called, "What the devil's going on out there?" then was lost in an explosion of coughs. Other lights appeared in other windows.

"Hold still!" McCutcheon commanded the stranger. "I swear I'll shoot you!"

"Don't!" the man begged. "I'm here as a friend . . . don't shoot me!"

McCutcheon knew right away that this was

not Jake Penn. The unfamiliar voice was clearly that of a young white man.

"Don't you hurt my Joe! Don't you dare shoot him!" Deborah cried out, lunging toward the terrified man in McCutcheon's gun sights.

Joe? Who was Joe, and why did Deborah . . . ?

It was suddenly clear. This surely was Joe Tifton, the young man he'd heard named as Deborah's lover from Hulltown. He'd come for a nocturnal tryst with his lover, and when Deborah had emerged from the house, it was not by chance. She'd been coming out to meet him.

Ben was the first out of the house, still hitching one gallus over his shoulder as he barreled out, shotgun in hand. Luke followed, staggering a little from a combination of lingering alcohol and interrupted sleep. Susanna was next. Jeremy and Marie remained at the door, and Mack pushed between them as the last one to exit. He was carrying the same Greener he'd carried when McCutcheon first saw him.

"Joe Tifton!" Ben exclaimed. "I'm damned if I ain't going to shoot you right here, you Harper-loving son of a—"

"Shut up, Ben, and put down that shotgun," Mack said. "You'll not shoot anybody. Joe, why are you here? You know I've forbidden you from coming around Deborah!"

Joe Tifton shifted from one foot to the other, then said, "No matter what you forbid, sir, I can't stay away from her. Especially at such a time as this."

Mack raised the Greener. "Joe, if you've so much as wrongly touched my daughter, I'll kill you myself before Ben gets the chance."

Deborah jumped between her father and lover. "Pa, he's never been anything but a gentleman to me! I swear it! He's here because he worries about me, Pa! He's been hiding out around our place, night after night, to guard the house!"

"What? Joe, is that true?"

"Yes, sir."

Mack stared at him in silence. McCutcheon was impressed. Joe Tifton truly must be a young man in love to do what he had.

Ben stepped forward, looking defiantly at Joe Tifton while he spoke. "He's a damned liar, Uncle Mack. Joe Tifton is a Harper-lover. Hangs about with Harpers all the time."

Joe Tifton spoke up. "Your feud ain't my feud, Ben. No reason it should be. I take no sides in such things. But I do love Deborah, and I'll not sit by and leave her unguarded when there's a murderer in this valley."

Ben lifted his shotgun and leveled it at Joe's head. "Let me blow his head off right now!" he said.

Deborah let out a scream and threw her arms around Joe.

"Put your gun down, Ben, right now," Mack

said. "Joe, you come inside. You and me need to talk."

"Send him away!" Ben said.

"I will," Mack said in a voice weak from the strain of coughing. "But not until I've heard more about this. Joe, if you've done what you say . . ."

"He has done it, Pa. And I've been sneaking him food and fresh clothes and such. I've told him not to do it, but he won't quit. He's looking out for me, Pa. Looking out for all of us, really," Deborah said.

Ben cursed and turned his back. McCutcheon knew what he was thinking: *outdone again.*

Luke said, "Tifton, you tell me: Have the Harpers hired this darky to kill us?"

"No, sir. They ain't. The Harpers believe that it's you Caywoods who hired him."

"That's loco!" Ben spat. "We wouldn't hire nobody to kill our own family!"

McCutcheon had to smile. A theory Ben deemed sensible when he was applying it to the Harpers was suddenly "loco" when turned around and applied to the Caywoods.

"The Harpers believe some of the stories of Caywood deaths are made up," Joe replied.

Ben swore. McCutcheon found this all almost funny.

"It seems more likely to me that whoever this

killer is has a grudge against both families," Mc-
Cutcheon cut in.

"Precisely so," Mack replied. "Joe, I'm going
to invite you in. Make no false assumptions
about it, though. I don't favor any association between you and Deborah, and I forbid it from
now on. But I believe your intentions are honor-
able and your actions courageous, even if they
are foolish."

McCutcheon noticed something odd about
Mack's manner and voice. He sounded weak and
trembly, and stood in a manner that indicated
something was hurting. His lungs, probably.

Ben swore again, then said, "Don't take him
in, Mack. And don't let him take *you* in! Joe
Tifton is a friend of the Harpers and I guarantee
you is here to spy on us. They're probably paying him to find out what we're saying and what
our plans are!"

"It ain't true, Mr. Caywood," Joe said with
conviction. "I'm here because I care about Deborah, that's all. I ain't trying to help the Harpers."

Mack nodded. "Come on inside, Joe. We'll
talk. Then, come morning, I'll find somebody to
take you back to Hulltown, where you belong. I
appreciate your concern for Deborah, but I can't
have you sneaking around my property anymore, no matter what the reason."

McCutcheon saw an opportunity. "I'll take
him to Hulltown in the morning, Mack," he said.

"Are you up to it with that wound?"

"John Mark stitched me up so good I don't think I'll have a problem at all. I'll go on to Hulltown with Mr. Tifton here, and find myself a doctor to take the stitches out in a day or two."

"You'll not come back to us?"

McCutcheon couldn't restrain a quick glance toward Susanna. "No, sir. I'll not be coming back. It's time for me to be moving on."

Mack tried to say something in reply, but was only able to cough. It was terrible to hear, the worst yet, and McCutcheon had the strong impression that Mack was growing much sicker, very fast.

Susanna went to her father, who stood leaning forward, coughing so badly it seemed he would retch.

"Pap, you feel fevered," she said. "You're hot."

"I'm fine, girl," he said in the weakest of voices. "Just leave me be." He coughed a couple more times, then slowly stood up straight again. "Let's get inside, out of this night air."

Chapter Seventeen

The next morning

McCutcheon couldn't help but like Joe Tifton, who traveled beside him along the narrow road that led to Hulltown.

McCutcheon had sat up with the family, listening to Joe talking openly about his devotion to Deborah, expressing his desire to someday marry her, and all in all presenting an image of himself that had McCutcheon wondering why Mack seemed so set against Joe. McCutcheon thought that if he had a daughter, Joe Tifton was just the kind of devoted young man he'd hope she'd marry.

Tifton also seemed to have plenty of common sense, urging the Caywoods to make peace with the Harpers so they could figure out together what was behind these murders. Ben had been vocal against this, and Luke had sat there silent and sullen, but on this matter Mack was ready to hear out Joe Tifton.

"I agree with you that it is immensely unlikely that these murders are being directly caused by the Harpers, and I know for sure they aren't being caused by us. The secret to this mystery lies somewhere in the past . . . something involving both families, and maybe not even related to the feud at all."

After Tifton's interrogation was finally over, Ben had insisted on sitting up all night to guard the "prisoner." Deborah wanted to be there as well, but Mack wouldn't let her. McCutcheon saw that Mack, in his way, could be as irrational and stubborn as Luke and Ben.

At that point he'd been glad that his departure from this family was imminent. All in all, this was a strange and troubled bunch.

All but Susanna. Among this group she gleamed like a jewel. It bothered McCutcheon to think of leaving and potentially never seeing her again.

When the excitement died down and most of the Caywoods returned to bed, McCutcheon had spent the remainder of the night in a worn, overstuffed chair in the front sitting room. He wanted to smoke a cigar but feared the smell might disturb some of the others trying to rest.

So he just listened to the ticking clock and tried to think warm and romantic thoughts about Emily, only to find he could think only of Susanna instead.

Early on in this journey toward Hulltown, Mc-Cutcheon had tried to start a conversation with Joe Tifton, but Tifton hadn't been in the mood. So McCutcheon settled for silence and watching the morning sun spill over the Caywood Valley, rendering beautiful and peaceful that which had seemed ominous and bleak in the night.

He'd left without saying good-bye to Susanna. It would have been too difficult to go otherwise.

An hour into the journey, Tifton abruptly spoke.

"Deb told me you helped Susanna out when she was in a gunfight with that killer."

"Yep. I was at the right place at the right time. Or the wrong place, depending on how you look at it."

"What brung you to these parts to start with?"

McCutcheon repeated the same old fable he'd used with the Caywoods.

"Yeah? Well, Deborah don't believe it. She told me so. She believes you're some kind of manhunter come looking for that murderer."

"When did she tell you that?"

"Yesterday afternoon. She brought me some bread and meat out behind the stable. She talked all about you and her notions about what you are."

"Deborah's got an active imagination."

"Are you a manhunter?"

McCutcheon was about to give another lie in

response, but suddenly he was tired of all that. He'd not been honest with anyone since he'd come here. Maybe it was time to give the truth a try. "In a way, I am a manhunter."

"No! Hired by who?"

"By nobody. I'm here for my own reasons. The truth is, I read about the killings in a newspaper story. The part about those 'Nora' letters left on the dead men caught my attention. I know a black man, you see, who has for years been on the hunt for his sister, Nora. They were slaves as children; they were separated, and he never saw her again, but has always been on the lookout for her."

Joe scrunched up his brows, thinking. "So . . . maybe he found out that something bad happened to Nora, and he decided to get revenge for it."

"That's what I'm thinking. Only there's one problem: Jake Penn is a highly moral man, not at all the kind to become a murderer. And yet . . ."

"What?"

"When I caught a glimpse of the man who put this bullet furrow in my side, it really did look like Jake."

"How good a look did you get?"

"Lightning light. Fast."

"Then maybe it was somebody who just looked like him. It would be hard to tell for sure by a lightning flash."

"I suppose."

Joe thought it all over a while. "If this is your friend, though, and he's getting vengeance for something that was done by the Caywoods or the Harpers, or both, it seems that somebody among them would recollect something that would give a clue to who Nora was and what this is all about."

"So it would seem. But so far I've not been able to find anyone among the Caywoods who remembers anything, or is willing to admit it, anyway."

"Maybe the Harpers will remember."

"You plan to ask some of them?"

"I might."

"Let me ask you a favor: If you do, don't mention the name of Jake Penn. I don't know that he's really involved, and I don't want to cause trouble for him that maybe he doesn't deserve."

"Well . . . all right. But you have to realize, Mr. McCutcheon, that if your friend does prove to be the killer, he's a threat to Deborah and therefore an enemy of mine. It's hard to be inclined to protect him."

"I understand. And if it turns out to be Jake who is guilty, then I can't ask you or anyone else to protect him. He'd deserve whatever punishment came to him." He paused. "But surely it isn't Jake. A man's character generally doesn't make such a complete turn."

"Unless he's discovered something so bad that it's shook him up to the point he ain't what he used to be."

McCutcheon was finding this subject painful, so he changed it. "What kind of town is Hulltown?"

Joe shrugged. "Not much of one, though it's where I've lived all my life. Some businesses, shops, a courthouse, houses, stables . . . all the usual, with nothing at all to make it stand out from any other sorry little town in this sorry little backwoods country."

"You don't speak too well of your home place."

"A fact's a fact. The only thing that makes this valley worth living in for me is Deborah. If I can ever get Mack to accept me so I can marry her. If he doesn't go along, I suppose I'll just have to steal her away and marry her somewhere else before he can find us and stop us."

"What's his concern about you, anyway?"

"He don't like any man who comes calling on his girls. He's got his stubborn side; all the Caywoods do. Mack is a more sober and sensible man than Ben or Luke or his late brother, Tom, but he's more like them than he realizes. And I can tell you this: He may talk against some of the things that Luke and Ben say, but down inside he's afraid they may be right. There's feud blood in his veins whether he wants to admit it or not. And these murders are just fueling the fire that's been burning in these hills as long as there's been Caywoods and Harpers here."

"So what will happen?"

"Either the murderer is caught soon, or things get even uglier between the Harpers and the Caywoods. The feud's been like a banked fire for the last few years: still hot, but not flaming. But that won't last. The fire is going to break out hotter than ever before long."

"Why won't the law help out? You'd think they'd be sweeping the woods for the killer."

"The local sheriff is married to a Harper, so as long as it was only the Caywoods being killed, he sat on his hands."

"But now the Harpers are dying, too."

"Yep. But I doubt you'll see much from the sheriff because of it. The Harpers like to handle law enforcement in their own way, if you know what I mean. And the sheriff is enough under their control—not to mention enough of a coward—to be glad to let them do the dirtier jobs. And that's bad news for the Caywoods. When I hide out around Mack's house, it ain't just that black murderer I've got an eye out for. I've been watching for Harpers, too."

"These Harpers sound rowdy and mean. But you have friends among them, you say."

Tifton shrugged. "They're like any other family. All kinds of folks in the bunch, some better and worse than others. For the most part, though, they're a devilish clan. There's some of them I don't mess with at all."

"Now that you've been run off by Mack, what will you do?"

"Stay gone a day or so, then go back. I love Deborah Caywood. As long as the Caywoods are in danger, I'll be haunting the woods around Mack's place, whatever Mack thinks about it. And don't take offense, sir, but if I see this black fellow show himself and I can get in a killing shot, I'll do it, even if he is your friend."

"I understand." And McCutcheon did. There was only so much defense a man could expect for his friends in such a grim situation as this one.

"How long until we reach Hulltown?" McCutcheon asked.

"We'll be coming up on it shortly after we top that second hill yonder."

"You know, I've been thinking," McCutcheon said. "If this killer isn't under the hire of either of the feuding families, then he must be taking care of himself in terms of food and so on. Maybe he's good at living off the land, but even so, it seems likely he'd have to resupply himself sometimes."

"You're thinking he might show up in Hulltown?"

"Maybe."

"I doubt it. Not at such a time as this. Any black stranger who shows his face around here right now would probably be shot down first with questions asked later."

Hulltown, as ugly as its name, finally showed itself. It was a brown, rough-edged, shapeless mass of a village, dominated by the rounded dome of the courthouse and one tall church steeple that might have been pretty once, but that now was blackened and unsightly because the church house to which it was attached was mostly burned down. The steeple itself looked like it could fall at any moment.

"Been pleased to meet you, Joe Tifton," Mc-Cutcheon said.

"Same here. Where will you go now?"

"I'll check into a hotel, if there is one." He didn't mention that the only reason he could afford a hotel was that Mack had slipped him some money as he left.

"There is. The Hulltown Hotel. Original kind of name, eh?"

"One name is as good as another as long as there's a roof and bed."

"You still going to keep looking for the killer?"

"Yes . . . though I don't have much notion about how."

"Take care of yourself."

"You, too. Especially when you go back into those woods, Joe. Watch out for that murderer, but also for Mack."

"I will."

They parted, and McCutcheon rode down the wide, dirty main street of Hulltown, Arkansas, looking for the hotel and thinking he'd never seen a more squalid place.

Part III

A Storm in the Hills

Chapter Eighteen

The Hulltown Hotel was a pleasant surprise. The exterior was unpainted, the siding gray and showing signs of dry rot here and there, but the interior was clean, the walls whitewashed, the furniture relatively new, the bed comfortable. McCutcheon stowed his possessions in the wardrobe and dresser. His horse was already lodged in the hotel stable.

He was hungry and headed for the street to find a café. He strode the boardwalk, taking in the town's rather pungent mixture of odors: dust, manure, smoke, lumber, stagnant rainbarrel water, horseflesh . . . sizzling steak. He focused on the latter and followed his nose toward a restaurant operating behind a big window of checkerboard glass and a broad oak door worthy of an English manor. A fine-looking establishment for so nondescript a town. Its name, emblazoned in white on the window, was, appropriately, THE OAKEN DOOR.

A man passed by McCutcheon on the boardwalk, caught his eye, tipped his hat. McCutcheon returned the gesture, and asked: "Is that café there worth eating at?"

"Oh, yes. Plain fare, but cooked very well. A little too much salt."

"I like salt. How'd they get so fine a front door?"

"The proprietor won it in a poker game. The door's worth more than the whole building, I've always been told. It came off some European castle, I think."

McCutcheon only half heard these last details. His attention had been caught by a sight on the other side of a window in a boot shop beside the café.

An elderly black man leaned over a workbench, working hard on tacking a new heel onto a boot. The remarkable thing was that he looked almost exactly like John Mark, so much so that McCutcheon thought for a couple of moments that he *was* John Mark. But it wasn't; this man had less hair, and was heavier-built.

McCutcheon might have gone in, struck up a conversation, and asked if there was a kinship between the old man and John Mark, but hunger called more loudly than curiosity.

The perfectly hung and balanced oaken door of the café opened without a sound. The scent of cooking steak was much more intense inside, and McCutcheon was soon parked at a table by

the checkerboard window, sipping coffee, nibbling fresh-sliced bread, and anticipating the arrival of the rare steak he'd just ordered.

He remembered the days when he and Jake
Penn had wandered around together with sometimes hardly two cents between them. In those
days visiting a restaurant such as this would
have been out of the question. He was grateful
all over again for the significant reward money
he and Penn had both earned in the Blain rescue
adventure south of the border. It was a better
thing to be well-fixed than impoverished.

But the freedom of drifting . . . ah, that had
been wonderful. On the move, no obligations, no
one else but himself and Jake to worry about
most of the time.

The steak arrived during the third cup of coffee, and McCutcheon began eating with the focused concentration of a hungry baby. As the
edge was knocked off his hunger, however, he
slowed down and began to examine the town
some more through one of the clear panes of the
window.

Specifically he eyed the burned-out ruin of the
church and the tall steeple that still loomed at its
front. Like the front door of this café, the steeple
seemed too fine, too ornate, for this little backwater. He wondered if the church would be re-
built, or if the steeple would simply stand there
alone, like a jilted bride, until finally the ele-

ments wore it away. It would be a shame for
such an architectural treasure to be lost. When
McCutcheon had been riding into town he'd
seen the steeple only from its blackened and
damaged rear; it had looked tottery and ruined.
Its front had been virtually untouched by the
flames, though, the impressive beauty still intact.
The tower looked sturdy enough from the front
to stand forever.

McCutcheon turned his attention to his plate
again and carved the last meat from the T-
shaped bone of his steak. When he looked out
the window again, it was just in time to see a big
man holding a pistol by the barrel, bring the butt
of the gun down toward the head of a signifi-
cantly smaller man he'd apparently just chased
down. The butt missed the man's head and hit
his shoulder instead. He let out a yell that Mc-
Cutcheon could hear loudly even behind the
window, then began swinging his fists at his at-
tacker. The man with the pistol pounded him
again and again, though, and despite never con-
necting with his noggin as intended, was doing a
lot of damage.

McCutcheon was out of his seat in moments.
He'd never been one to watch a big man bully a
little one, no matter what the dispute. He was
out the big oaken door in a flash, followed by
two other men from the restaurant.

Intervention was unnecessary, though. By the

time McCutcheon and the others were at the edge of the boardwalk, a man with a badge was on the scene, pushing the two fighters apart and drawing his pistol.

"That's enough, Emo Harper!" he yelled at the bigger man. "No more of that!"

"Out of the way, Sheriff!" the man yelled back. "I'll kill this squat bastard!"

"No, sir, you won't. You'll not commit a murder right here in the street, Emo! I'll not stand for that!"

One of the men who had come out of the restaurant with McCutcheon yelled out, "Why not, Sheriff? He's a Harper! I thought you always let the Harpers have their way with the Caywoods!"

The sheriff, jostling with the two fighters, pretended not to hear, though a fast and angry glance fired toward the boardwalk betrayed that he had.

"That's a Harper and a Caywood fighting?" McCutcheon asked the man.

"Hell, yes. That sorry feud's heating up again, thanks to all the murders." The man glanced at McCutcheon. "You not from around here?"

"From Texas. But I've heard about the murders. And the feud."

The sheriff finally had the pair calming down a bit. The big Harper turned over his pistol to the

sheriff, but only after eliciting a promise that he
could pick it up on his way back out of town.

"Wonder what they're fighting about?" Mc-
Cutcheon asked.

"Skunk Caywood there probably said something cross to Emo Harper. That's all it takes to
set someone off sometimes . . . especially if
you're a Harper."

"Is Skunk Caywood part of the Mack Caywood branch of the family?"

"Not close, I don't think. But they're all related, and the sorry Harpers hate them all."

"You don't like the Harpers much, I take it."

"I can't say I really like either family. Their
feud has done a lot to hurt this whole region. But
of the two the Harpers are by far the worst.
Sorry, mean, treacherous, selfish, violent bunch
of curs and bitches. I hope you ain't a relation."

Candid fellow, McCutcheon thought. "Don't
worry. I'm not a relation. What kind of fellow is
the sheriff there?"

"In the pockets of the Harpers. He puts on a
show of being fair, but in the end it's the Harpers
he caters to. He's married into their family, and I
swear I believe they've paid him off on the side
to boot."

"Will he ever catch that murderer out in the
mountains?"

"He didn't half try when it was just Caywoods
being killed. Now there's some dead Harpers,

too. He'll have to perform now, and actually go out and catch that murdering darky."

"As I hear it, that killer is like a ghost. Can't get your hands around him. Not the kind of man you want to have to chase."

The man chuckled. "I'll bet our good sheriff there is thinking that same thought every waking moment."

"Let me change the subject a second," McCutcheon said. "Who's the old man who fixes shoes in this shop over here?"

"Old Barnabas? Well, he's just . . . Old Barnabas. Been around this town longer than God."

"Has he got family?"

"A brother, name of John Mark, I think. He works over on the Mack Caywood spread."

John Mark's brother! McCutcheon could have guessed it from looks alone.

He decided to play ignorant a little and see if this man might know anything he'd like to know himself. "Hey, is it true that there's some kind of note or sign or something that's been left on the bodies of the dead men?"

"Yeah. Something about vengeance for a woman named Nora," McCutcheon's companion replied.

"Who's Nora?"

"Nobody seems to know. Everybody figures that she must be somebody who was around here years ago, because nobody remembers noth-

ing about anything involving a Nora that I know
of." The man paused, thinking. "I wonder if anybody's asked Old Barnabas? He knows more
about things that happened a long time ago than
anybody else."

"If he knows something, why hasn't he come
forward?" McCutcheon said.

"Maybe nobody's bothered to ask him,"
replied the other.

Chapter Nineteen

The sheriff sent the interrupted brawlers off in two different directions, and stuck the seized pistol of Emo Harper under his belt.

"How long until you give him that pistol back, Sheriff?" McCutcheon's big-talking companion called. "Until you're out of sight around the corner? You going to shine his boots for him, too?"

The sheriff fired a dark glare the man's way. "You'd best learn to nail down that flapping tongue, Bill. You want me to run you in?"

"Why, what have I done wrong, Sheriff? I'm just an American citizen exercising my right to free speech. I ain't committed no crimes . . . like, say, taking a payoff as a public official."

The sheriff glared all the more darkly, but didn't say anything more. He turned and stalked away, shoulders back in an attempt to look manly, but all in all he came across more like a man in a hurry to reach the outhouse.

McCutcheon's companion laughed loudly after him. "See you later, Sheriff! Hey, when you going to bring in that killer? The county's waiting!"

The sheriff didn't turn or reply. He got out of sight as quickly as he could.

"There's one scared man," McCutcheon observed. "Is he the only law here? There's no town marshal?"

"He's all there is. Sorry state of affairs, huh? That's why folks here pretty much try to handle their own problems and the devil take the law."

The café door opened behind them and the proprietor appeared. "Are you gentlemen prepared to settle your bills?" he asked with a tight smile.

"Of course . . . sorry," McCutcheon said, digging into his pocket. "I wasn't planning to stiff you."

He paid for his meal, went back in to get his coat and hat, and returned to the boardwalk. The other man had by then also settled up and gone his own way.

McCutcheon winced and rubbed his side. The stitches John Mark had given him were itching badly. He wondered when he should have them removed. Tomorrow, maybe. He'd have to find a doctor.

McCutcheon walked next door to the shoe shop, but Old Barnabas was no longer behind the window, and the door was locked. He must have left while McCutcheon was eating.

McCutcheon walked through Hulltown slowly, thinking.

The matter of those Nora references on the bodies of the slain . . . everyone seemed to assume that the reference must be to something long ago, because no one could associate the name with any incidents of more recent years.

But if the Nora in question was Jake Penn's Nora, whatever incident it was couldn't be too many years in the past. Jake was in his middle years, but not an old man, and his sister would be the same general age.

So maybe the Nora matter, whatever it was, wasn't forgotten because it was too old, but because it was too obscure. Or maybe buried too deeply by those with a reason to keep it hidden for the sake of someone's reputation or safety. Or maybe the Nora in reference wasn't Jake Penn's Nora at all.

Whatever had happened to the mysterious Nora must have been terrible indeed to be worth such a fearsome vengeance.

The more McCutcheon thought about it, the more depressed he became.

He walked the streets for hours, going nowhere, knowing no one, and suffering under a great, heavy burden of foreboding he couldn't fully account for.

When he'd wandered until he'd seen every square yard of Hulltown at least three times, he

went to a general store and bought paper, an en-
velope, a pencil, and a long, cheap cigar, then returned to his hotel room. He lit a lamp, then the
cigar, and stared at the blank paper before him
for several minutes.

He lifted the pencil and began to write.

Dear Emily . . .

What followed were paragraphs of pure hon-
esty. McCutcheon told Emily of the newspaper
article he had read, of all that had happened to
him since his departure, and his fearful suspi-
cions that the murderer in the Ozark hills might
be none other than his old companion Jake Penn.
He told her of the Caywoods, and of Susanna,
and of his rising doubts that he was truly ready
to marry. He worried as he wrote that he was
being *too* honest . . . but how could a man be too
honest with a woman he had promised to spend
the rest of his life with?

But as he finished the letter, McCutcheon
knew that he could no longer spend his life with
Emily. Something had changed in the brief time
he had been away from her . . . no, not so much
changed as become clear. He had realized that
what he felt for Emily was indeed love, but not
the kind of love that leads a man to marry.
Perhaps someday it might turn into that, but it
wasn't there yet.

Nor was he sure he wanted it to be. Not with
Susanna Caywood in the world.

It was loco, he realized. He hardly knew Susanna, and what he did know of her wasn't entirely positive. She was willful, stubborn, downright bossy. Willing to take foolish risks, too, and seemingly not inclined to let herself appear subservient to any man to even the slightest degree.

Surely she didn't love him. He wasn't sure how much she even liked him.

Yet he couldn't stop thinking about her . . . and it was downright difficult to keep his mind on Emily.

When the letter was finished he stared at it. Dare he send it?

To do so would be to throw away any chance at a life with Emily and Martin. Emily had been hurt in romance once; she would not continue a romance with a man who was uncertain about her.

He would also be throwing aside a good career as a merchant in Whitefield. But did he even want that career? He'd thought he did, just as he'd thought he wanted Emily as his wife.

Maybe he *did* want it . . . maybe he *did* want Emily for his wife . . .

Blast it! This whole situation was somewhat like that church steeple outside, which was unappealing from one angle of view, beautiful from another. The perspective made all the difference.

He folded the letter and put it into a drawer.

He'd not mail it yet. Not until he'd figured things out a little better.

McCutcheon went out and bought himself a supper that he hardly tasted. He was depressed, seriously considering taking a bottle back to his room and getting drunk. He knew it wasn't a good idea, but he did go so far as buying a bottle. Maybe he'd drink it, maybe not.

Who was he fooling? Of course he'd drink it.

Back in his room, he stood by the window with the light out, looking across the dark street below and wondering what was to become of him. How in the world had he managed to fall in love with a virtual stranger, one who probably hadn't given him a thought since he left Mack Caywood's place?

He sighed, then looked toward the steeple at the burned out church.

For a moment, a light flickered within it. Just a flash, barely detectable, as if someone had carried a lamp past a small window in the wall of the steeple. The light had not been at the top of the steeple, but about halfway down it.

McCutcheon watched the steeple another two or three minutes, but saw the light flicker no more. Maybe it had just been some odd reflection. He didn't recall seeing windows in the side of the steeple, at least not at that level.

Putting it down as a mistake of perception or just an unexplainable oddity, he went to his bed and lay down on his back, staring at the ceiling and thinking about Susanna Caywood.

He reached for the bottle. He'd not drink too much, just enough to knock the edge off this dark mood of his.

Or maybe he'd drink until he was numb. Then he'd sleep, and for a few blessed hours, push the confusing world away.

Chapter Twenty

Midmorning, the following day

Susanna Caywood strode down the hallway and stopped outside the doorway of her father's bedroom. She glanced up at the clock on the wall, then put her ear nearly against the door, listening while idly touching her still-tender arm in its sling.

Near silence . . . though she could hear him breathing, for which she was thankful. She'd actually began to wonder if he might be lying dead in there.

Marie came down the hall, looking at her sister with her eternally sad-looking eyes. "Did you hear him coughing last night?" Marie asked in a whisper.

"Yes . . . it's never been so bad. I tried to go in and see how he was—"

"But he wouldn't let you in? Yes . . . he did the same with me. He's so stubborn."

"We're all stubborn, Marie, at least most of us are. It's a Caywood trait."

"He's alive, isn't he?"

"Yes, I can hear his breathing . . . but it's so ragged and rough."

An explosion of coughing erupted on the other side of the door, followed by a loud groan from Mack Caywood.

"He sounds bad, Susanna."

Jeremy appeared like a small ghost, coming silently through a nearby doorway. "Is Uncle Mack all right?"

"I don't think he is, Jeremy. I think he's gotten a lot sicker," Susanna replied.

"He won't die, will he?" Jeremy spoke in a quivering voice, nearly ready to cry. He was that way most of the time these days, and it made Susanna angry, not at Jeremy, but at the terrible situation in which the family existed. She never hated the unknown murderer more than when she saw what the killings had done to her innocent young cousin. Jeremy might never be the same again, she feared. He was just too young to have to be enduring this.

"No, Jeremy. He won't die. But I think he might need to see a doctor. Maybe even go to a hospital somewhere."

"Oh, he won't want to do that," Marie said. "You know he hates doctors and hospitals. He'll just want John Mark to take care of him."

"John Mark is good, but some things require a real physician," Susanna replied. "If I have to, I'll ask Ben or Luke to go to Hulltown and bring Dr. Leedman back to examine him."

"Ben is gone, and Uncle Luke, too," Jeremy said.

"*Gone?* Where?"

"I don't know," Jeremy replied, voice quivering worse because Susanna had reacted intensely to what he said. "I saw them riding away together an hour ago."

"Where could they be going?" Marie asked.

Susanna bit her lip and frowned. "I have a notion . . . God, I hope I'm wrong. I've heard Ben talking to Luke lately . . . foolish talk, about trying to unify all the scattered Caywood family and 'end' the feud by winning it. But I didn't think the fool would actually try to do it!"

"Maybe that's not what they're doing," Marie said. "I hope it's not . . . I couldn't stand it if the feud broke out into real fighting again. I couldn't stand it at all!"

Mack coughed more, then mumbled something that sounded incoherent.

"I'm going in there," Susanna said. "I think he's really sick this time."

"The door's locked, Susanna."

"I know." She reached into the pocket of the apron she wore. "But since Pa got so sick I've always made a point of keeping a key to this door myself for fear of just such a situation as this."

"He won't like you having a key to his room. You know how he is."

"I think he's sick enough that he won't know anything." Susanna clicked the lock and pushed open the door.

Mack was spread across his bed, the covers a mess, his face red and dripping with sweat, his hair matted. The unmistakable stench of high fever filled the room. He'd retired to his bed even before sunset the day before, something he never did except when he was very ill, and obviously he had worsened greatly through the night.

Susanna ran to the bed and put her hand on Mack's damp brow. He looked at her blearily but showed no reaction; at the moment he probably could tell no difference between reality and the illusions of his fever.

"He's burning up," Susanna said tightly. "Dear Lord . . . I've never seen such a fever before."

"He's going to die!" Jeremy wailed. "He'll be dead just like my father!"

"He won't be dead! Now hush! And hold yourself together, Jeremy. You have to be strong until our difficult times are over. Otherwise you just add to the problem."

"Don't speak so sternly to the boy, Susanna!" Marie rebuked.

"Stern is what is called for right now. Jeremy, go bring in John Mark. Tell him that my father is very sick, and to fetch some of his feverroot."

Jeremy nodded and darted out.

Susanna went to the wash basin and soaked a cloth in cool water, then bathed her father's brow. His eyes were half open, staring through slits at nothing in particular. His chest wheezed and rattled and she wondered how a man could have worsened so much, so quickly.

Susanna bathed his brow again and again, and prayed harder than she ever had before.

Chapter Twenty-one

Jim McCutcheon opened his eyes, then shut them again quickly, groaning.

Why had he done it? What good had a night of drinking done him? If he'd felt good late last night, he couldn't remember it now. All he could feel was pain.

After a time he opened his eyes again, very slowly, and managed to look at his pocketwatch on the bedstand beside him. Nearly noon! He couldn't believe he'd slept so long.

His throbbing brain for a time couldn't register much except discomfort. He strained to remember the details of the prior day. Just what had he done that had gotten him depressed enough to get so drunk?

"Oh, no."

He sat up, too fast. It was like being kicked in the forehead. He winced, held still, then got up weakly.

That letter to Emily. He couldn't remember

everything that was in it, but he knew it had been brutally honest.

Had he mailed it?

As speedily as his physical state would allow, he began searching the room. With deep relief he located the letter.

He sat down and took several deep breaths. Thank God it hadn't been mailed! Today he wasn't sure he was quite so ready to burn all his bridges. He was as unsure as ever about his future with Emily, but it was surely foolish to think he had any part in Susanna's life. A bit of mutual male/female tension, some conversation . . . that's all there was.

Besides, he'd made a promise to return to Emily, and to Martin. It was his obligation to keep it.

He tore the letter into pieces and tossed them into the trash can, then lay down several more minutes, vowing never to drink again.

When he felt like he could handle it, he got up, washed and dressed himself, and headed out in search of coffee and maybe a bit of toast. The thought of ingesting anything more than that was too much to endure.

Luke had fallen behind again, and Ben turned in the saddle to see why. He was just in time to see Luke hurriedly slipping a metal flask into his pocket.

"Luke, damn it, you told me you'd do no drinking today!"

"I'm sorry, Ben. But I need it, for strength."

"You'll get no strength that way. We need clear heads for what we're doing. We've got a job of persuasion before us that might be challenging. Why don't you give me the flask?"

Luke's temper flashed, but he didn't let it show. It was humiliating enough to be so weak-kneed that he was being bossed around by his own young and rather immature nephew. But he'd not give up his flask like some schoolboy having contraband seized by the schoolmaster!

"I'll keep my flask," he said. "I'll not drink from it again."

"Luke, you ain't the strongest when it comes to resisting temptation. Why don't you just go ahead and give it—"

"Damn it, Ben, I'm keeping my flask! I'm going along with you here because I think you're right, but don't get the notion you're my mother! You hear me?"

Ben nodded. He would say no more about it. He knew and respected the unusual dynamic that existed between him and his alcoholic uncle. Ben's personality was forceful, somehow intimidating to Luke despite Luke being the elder. Luke had fought in the late war, had endured his share of barroom brawls as a young man, and had engaged in some feud-related skirmishes

that made for hair-curling adventure stories . . .
but liquor had taken a toll. Most of the time Luke
was a weak and easily intimidated man. But at
times the stronger Luke of old would assert himself, as had happened just now, and when Luke
and Mack had argued so forcefully earlier on.

"Just don't get no notions that you can be the
boss man here," Luke said, all but snarling at
Ben. "A man's got his pride, you know."

"All right, Luke. All right. I'm sorry. I just
want to make sure this goes like it should. Damn
it, I've lost a father and I want to make sure the
Harpers pay for it. I don't want to mess this up."

Luke calmed down. "Yeah. Yeah. I know.
Don't worry. I'll not drink too much."

Ben grinned and the worst of the tension was
over.

"How do you think they'll respond to us,
Luke?"

Luke shrugged. "Can't say . . . but I think
they'll be willing to join us. Michael Caywood
has never struck me as one to sit by and do nothing."

Ben nodded. "Good."

Michael Caywood was a distant cousin. Ben
and Luke were heading for his home, now about
a mile ahead, hoping to begin the process of
building a family army that would bring to an
end the long feud—and the murders that Ben

and Luke had persuaded themselves were feud-related—with a resounding Caywood victory.

Having Michael Caywood join them would be an important victory in itself. Michael was the perceived head of one branch of the Caywood family, just as Mack headed a different branch. With Michael's influence, Caywoods from all across the mountain country would unify against the Harpers. The prospect made Ben's heart beat fast with passionate hope.

"I'll be damned . . ." Luke muttered the words as he looked toward the horizon past Ben.

"What is it?" Ben followed his uncle's gaze, and discovered the answer to his own question.

Smoke was rising, thick and black, a couple of ridges over.

"That looks like the smoke of a house fire," Ben observed.

"Yes," replied Luke. "And it's coming from the direction of Michael's place."

Ben and his uncle looked at one another a moment in stunned silence, pondering the possibilities.

"Let's go," Ben said.

Luke seemed oddly reluctant. "I don't know I want to go there . . ."

"What? What are you talking about, Luke? We've come all this way for the very reason of seeing Michael. Besides, if his house is afire, he may need our help."

Luke, staring at the smoke, had gone pale. Ben wondered what could be going through is uncle's mind.

"Come on, Luke. We've got to go on."

Luke nodded slowly, without enthusiasm.

They rode off together. Luke, staying behind his nephew a little, managed to sneak out the flask and take a nervous swallow without Ben noticing.

Chapter Twenty-two

Several cups of coffee and half a loaf of toasted bread took the edge off McCutcheon's hangover. The headache would die slowly and reluctantly through the day, he supposed, but he was past the worst of it. He could go on.

He left the restaurant, glanced at the nearest saloon, and whispered a curse on all alcohol.

He scratched lightly at his side. Those stitches John Mark had put in were growing annoying. They'd done their job well, though; his wound was already far along the way to a thorough healing.

He'd have the stitches removed tomorrow. Even later today, if the itching got worse.

He passed the window of the shoe shop and noticed motion inside. He squinted in, then went to the door and opened it. A bell attached to the top jangled as he walked in.

Old Barnabas was in the rear, talking with an equally elderly white man in a leather apron. The latter turned and approached McCutcheon, looking at him through a mass of white eyebrows that drooped down over the cavities of his eyes.

"Help you, young man?"

"I'd like to see Mr. Barnabas there, if he's available."

Old Barnabas looked up with a curious expression. His resemblance to John Mark was stronger than ever.

"All righty," the white man said. "Barnabas . . . a visitor for you."

Old Barnabas tottered up to the front of the store as the other old man tottered back.

"Good morning, sir," Old Barnabas said. "What can I do for you?"

"How are you at stitching, Mr. Barnabas?"

"Well, I do right fine at it, sir. I've stitched up many a boot and shoe in my day."

"Good stitching runs in the family, then."

"Beg your pardon?"

"You have a brother named John Mark."

"Yes, sir, I do." Old Barnabas abruptly looked troubled. "Oh, tell me, sir, there ain't nothing wrong with him, is there?"

"No. No, not at all. Not as of day before yesterday, anyway. I saw him then."

"You was at the Caywood place, sir?"

"I was. As a matter of fact, John Mark was very helpful to me while I was there. I'd gotten a cut along my side, and he stitched me up."

Old Barnabas grinned. "So that's the stitching you were talking about. John Mark is as good as a physician. That's what people say."

"Listen, I wanted to talk to you a few minutes, if I can." He cut his eyes toward the man in the back. "In private."

"Well, sir, I reckon we can do that." Barnabas nodded toward the front door.

Outside on the boardwalk, Old Barnabas folded his arms and looked at McCutcheon with an expression both inquisitive and cautious.

"I want to tell you something about why I came to Arkansas and see if you might have some information to help me," McCutcheon said. He briefly related his background, as far back as Texas, at least, and told of his journey and of how he managed to get the furrow in his side. By that point he had Barnabas's rapt attention.

He paused, then decided to be as honest with Barnabas as he had with Joe Tifton. "When I was at the Caywood house, I told all of them, including your brother, that I had come there in pursuit of a man who had stolen my horse. That was a lie. My horse had actually died on me right after I got into Arkansas. The truth is that I came to Arkansas because I'd read a story in a newspaper about the murderer out in these mountains, and how he left the words

'Vengeance for Nora' on the corpses of those he killed.

"Up until I settled down in Texas and got my-self engaged to be married, I'd been a partner for a good while with a man named Jake Penn. A black man, by the way. The whole time I was with him, Jake was a man with a mission. He'd been separated from his sister when they were both young slaves, and he's spent a big part of his adult years searching for her."

Barnabas said, "And I'm going to guess her name is Nora."

"That's right. So you can imagine what I thought when I read that there was a black man killing people hereabouts and leaving notes about a Nora . . ."

Barnabas nodded. "Yes, sir. I do see."

"I didn't tell the Caywoods the real reason I'd come because I wasn't sure how they'd react to having a man among them who just might be the friend and one-time drifting partner of the very man killing their kin. But I'm telling you the full story in hopes that maybe you'll know something. They tell me that you know the lore of this area better than any man alive."

"I suppose I do know a lot of things, sir."

"Then maybe the name Nora rings a bell with you. Or the name Jake Penn."

"Sir, let me ask you a question: Do I look to you like a wicked man?"

McCutcheon was surprised by that query. "No. Not at all."

"I think I must, sir. Otherwise you wouldn't have asked me what you did."

McCutcheon wondered if he'd somehow offended this old man unintentionally. "I don't understand."

"If I knew who Nora was, sir, and why these murders were happening, do you think I'd not have already told it?"

"Well . . . I suppose you would."

"For otherwise, if I didn't tell it, I'd be a mighty wicked man. To know such a thing and not tell it would be wrong."

"I understand your point. My intention wasn't to insult you, Barnabas. I just hoped maybe something I said would jar a memory that hadn't come forth before."

"I don't believe you've told me what your name is, sir."

"Haven't I? I beg your pardon . . . I'm James McCutcheon. Just call me Jim."

"I feel more comfortable with Mr. McCutcheon, if it's all the same to you, sir."

"Fine. But I take it you have nothing to tell me."

"As I said, sir: If I knowed anything, I'd have told it by now. The Caywoods are a family I don't want harm to come to. My brother's been part of them for years and years. You hurt a

Caywood and you hurt John Mark. You hurt John Mark, and you hurt Old Barnabas."

"Yes, sir. That's the way it should be with brothers."

"The fact is, sir, long before you came here today, I've gone through my mind time and again, trying to remember any Nora, or anything that happened to a Nora that would cause somebody to do the wicked things that have been done here lately. And I can't remember a thing. Nothing at all."

"You've never known a Nora in these parts?"

"Yes. I've known two, as I can recollect. One the wife of a shopkeeper who left here about ten years ago. The other a preacher's daughter who married a gentleman from Mississippi and moved away. And there may have been a third Nora, but my memory is no good on that one. This was a woman married to a Negro tenant farmer out in the Caywood Valley many years ago. He got into trouble with the law and was hauled off to jail. By that time, the woman had died."

"How did she die?"

Barnabas looked away and for some reason did not answer readily. "A fire," he finally said.

"Was this Nora, if that was her name, a Negro woman?"

"She was, sir. I didn't know her well, nor her husband. He wasn't the kind of man you'd want to know, to tell the truth. Mighty unfriendly. You come around close to his place and he'd run you off with a shotgun."

McCutcheon was intrigued. "Did you ever talk to him?"

"No, sir."

"How about his wife?"

"One time, sir. I met her out on the road, walking along from the creek carrying laundry back toward her cabin in a basket. I recall she was crying about something or another, and she talked to us some. I don't recall nothing except that she was sorrowing over something her husband had done, and how she wished she'd never married him because he treated her mean. I talked kindly to this woman and went on my way and she went on hers. That was that, and I don't know I'd recall any of it, either, if not for the fact that she was a right pretty woman, and I always remember pretty women." Barnabas grinned and winked. "But I don't always remember the name, and I can't swear her name was Nora."

"What about her husband's name?"

"Can't remember. But I'll study back on it and see if it comes to mind. Won't do you much good, though, that I can see. He's long gone from here."

"Yes . . . unless he's come back."

"I see what you mean, sir."

McCutcheon shook Old Barnabas' hand. "Thank you for your help. If you do remember anything more, you can find me at the Hulltown Hotel, room 204."

"You want me to say anything you said to John Mark, if I see him? He comes by on rare occasion when he's in Hulltown."

"Go ahead and tell him. He and the Caywoods were good to me and I feel bad I lied to them as it is. And ask him how Susanna is doing."

"Yes, sir."

McCutcheon turned away, ready to go and sorry this meeting hadn't been more productive.

Barnabas asked, "Sir . . . what did you say the name of your old partner is?"

McCutcheon looked at him over his shoulder. "Jake Penn. Does that name mean anything to you?"

"Jake Penn . . . Jake Penn. No, no. I wish I could say it did, but I don't believe it does."

"You sure?"

"I think so." Barnabas had a slight frown as he said it. McCutcheon noted it and made plans to see Barnabas again before he left Hulltown.

"Good day to you, Barnabas."

"And to you, too, sir."

Barnabas stood on the boardwalk and watched McCutcheon depart.

"Jake Penn," Barnabas muttered to himself, a

man trying to free a lost memory from a long-closed mental cage. Or maybe it wasn't a memory at all. Still, there was something about that name . . .

"Jake," he muttered again. "Jake."

He shook his head and went back into the shop, glowering in thought.

Chapter Twenty-three

Michael Caywood, though a relative of Luke and Ben Caywood, had never been particularly close to either, or to any of the other Caywoods of Mack's branch of the family. As families will do, the Caywood clan had spread out across the county over time, putting distance between themselves in more than the geographic sense. Ultimately, though, the Caywoods retained a sense of kinship, more so than most families, a process encouraged by the fact they all possessed a common enemy in the Harper family. If any of them ever tended to forget they were Caywoods, there was always some insult-flinging, or fist-swinging, Harper who would show up and remind them.

Still, in recent years, when the feud had been more of a symbolic than actual reality and significant violence between the feuding clans had been confined mostly to the occasional saloon fistfight, the bond between the Caywoods had grown thin. Luke Caywood still threw up his hand in a wave when he happened to see Michael Caywood or some of Michael's brothers in Hulltown, but there was no crossing the street to talk or any real interest in what was going on in one another's branches of the family.

Today, though, as Luke and Ben rode up to see the flaming remains of what had been Michael Caywood's moderately sized but excellent log house, Michael might as well have been one of their immediate kin. The Caywood family bond was a palpable thing even as Michael, his eyes dark with fury and sorrow, turned to watch his distant cousins ride up.

Ben swung lithely out of his saddle while Luke dismounted a bit more slowly. Ben strode up to Michael, nodded a curt hello, then indicated the burning building.

"Harpers?"

"Yep," Michael replied. "Seen 'em myself. So did Kate." Kate was his wife, who stood beside him, weeping, with children clinging to her dirty dress.

"How many?"

"Five."

Luke reached them, and the same information was briefly repeated for his benefit. Luke nodded, very pale.

"I ain't seen such as this for twenty years," Ben said. "Last time the Harpers burned out a Caywood was back when Enoch Caywood's place got torched. I wasn't even born at the time."

"I remember," Michael said. "I was just a boy at the time, but I remember it well. You remember it, too, I'm sure, Luke."

Luke looked ghastly, staring at the flames. He did not seem to hear the question.

Neither Ben nor Michael mentioned, or even remembered, that there had never been any definite proof that the Harpers had actually set fire to the Enoch Caywood residence—nothing more than a woodland shack. Forgotten as well was that Enoch had been an even harder drinker than Luke and had managed to nearly set his shack on fire all by himself at least three times earlier.

Ben watched the flames eating away the last of Michael's house and said, "Nobody in your family hurt, I hope?"

"No. But the children had a bunch of new kittens they was playing with. No more kittens now, and the mama cat's dead, too." He spat on the ground. "Damned Harpers. As far as I'm concerned, there ain't a Harper breathing who's worth more than one of them dead kittens."

Ben looked solemnly at Michael. "I'm glad to hear you say that, Michael. Luke and me have come calling today because of the Harpers. You know what they're saying about us, don't you?"

"That the murderer in the hills is under the hire of Caywoods."

"Exactly. A damned lie. In my opinion it's the exact opposite that's the truth. The Harpers have hired a killer, faked some deaths among their own kin, and begun a new assault on the Caywoods." Ben had repeated the story to himself and others so many times that he now actually believed it and could say it with a conviction that was quite persuasive, especially to a man in the current emotional state of Michael Caywood.

"I believe you, Ben. I believe it's true as gospel, sure as I'm a Christian."

"It ain't right, Michael. The Caywoods have tried hard to put an end to the feud, and the Harpers just won't let it go." Again Ben spoke with persuasive intensity, spewing words possessing only a small percentage of truth at best. Mack Caywood had tried to end the feud, it was true, but there had been little help from any other Caywood. And it was Ben as much as any Harper who refused to let the feud die.

"Why did you come to see me?" Michael asked.

"We came to ask your help in getting all us scattered Caywoods to working together again. The Harpers are out to destroy us all, and we've got to band together if we're going to overcome it. We're ready to win this old feud once and for all. If the Harpers want a fight, we're ready to take it to them." He waved toward the burning structure. "This to me says they do indeed want a fight. This is a declaration of war."

Michael nodded. There were a few details that he'd neglected to mention: about some livestock belonging to some Harpers that he'd allowed to mingle in with his own, some brands that had been subtly altered, and a few rash threats he himself had uttered, when under the influence of alcohol, to a gaggle of Harpers in a saloon a few miles from here. There was also some reason to believe that the Harpers who had paid call on him today hadn't come intending to burn his house, but only his barn. It had been Michael's own bullet, fired from his bedroom window at the creeping Harpers, that had shattered the lantern one was carrying toward the barn, igniting some rubbish with a blaze that spread quickly to the house. Michael did not let these details linger in his mind, though; it was much easier and more satisfying to see himself as the fully wronged party.

"What do you aim to do about this, Michael?" Ben asked.

Michael faced his visitors squarely. "I'd like to do the very thing you came to talk to me about. I'd like to round up my brothers and cousins. Get some rifles and shotguns and ammunition together, and go pay call on a few Harpers. There'll be more houses burned in this county today."

Ben grinned and pounded Michael's shoulder. They'd just gone from being distant kin to the closest of allies. "Good man. Good man. It's time the Caywoods got their vengeance. My father was murdered by that damned Harper killer, Michael. You knew that, I suppose."

"I did. I'm sorry. He was a good man." In fact, Michael had hardly known Tom Caywood.

Ben turned to grin at Luke. This fire, unfortunate as it was for Michael and his family, had been a fortuitous occurrence for their cause. It would be easy now to round up an army of angry Caywoods. The Harpers were about to suffer greatly.

Luke was looking ill. He returned to his horse on the pretext of looking for something in his saddlebags, but actually it was to take another much-needed swig on his flask.

"Were you able to rescue any of your weapons from the fire, Michael?"

"My rifle and my shotgun, most of my ammunition. And I've got an old pistol stored in grease over in the storeroom of my barn."

"Let's get all that together and go find some of your brothers."

Michael nodded. He seemed animated now, almost happy despite the loss of his home. "I'm glad you fellows came here today, Ben. I believe God himself must have sent you. It's indeed time we put a stop to the Harpers and their ways.

They want a war, they've got a war." He paused
to beam approvingly at Ben. "You've grown up
to be quite a man, Ben. Quite a leader. I always
thought of Mack as the leader of your branch of
the family. Maybe you're moving up to take the
job."

Ben tried to look humble, but he liked what
Michael had just said. Mack was getting older
and sicker and had for a long time been too eager
for peace. It was time the Caywoods followed a
different course.

Over on the horizon, clouds were beginning to
gather, very slowly. Luke took another quick sip
from his flask and watched them. It might
amount to nothing, or it could be the start of
what would become a major storm before night-
fall. He put the cork back in the flask.

He didn't like the look of that darkening distant sky. In the immediate context, clouds on the
horizon seemed a bad omen.

Luke looked again at the burning house. The
whole situation brought to mind a thing he
didn't like to remember . . . a fire from years ago,
the smell of burning wood and hay, the terrible
noise made by horses trying in vain to escape the
flames . . . the even more horrible noises made by
human beings similarly trapped . . .

He shuddered and tried to erase the image,
but it lingered. He unstoppered the flask again
and turned it up.

Chapter Twenty-four

Jim McCutcheon had made a decision: It was time to give up his quest.

It was clear to him now that he wasn't likely to discover on his own whether the killer in the hills was really Jake Penn. Not unless he wanted to put himself out as bait and see who came to bite. This was not an appealing prospect.

McCutcheon looked beyond the borders of the squalid town and watched the horizon darken. Too early to tell, but there might be bad weather later today.

A worsening itch in his stitched-up side made McCutcheon wince. Time to get these stitches removed, he decided.

He inquired of a man on the street the location of the local physician's office and discovered that the doctor practiced only two buildings down from the hotel. The doctor was just descending the stairs from his upstairs office when McCutcheon approached.

"Doc?"

"Yes. My name is Leedman."

"The name's McCutcheon . . . I've got some stitches need removing."

"Just on my way to get a bite to eat."

"I'm itching something awful, Doc."

The middle-aged physician sighed, smiled, and nodded for McCutcheon to follow him back into the office.

"That looks like a bullet furrow," Leedman observed after McCutcheon removed his shirt.

"It is. A hunting accident." Lying was less troublesome than the truth just now.

"You're lucky. A different angle and you might be dead. Who stitched you up?"

"Did it myself." One good lie deserved another.

"You did a good job of it."

McCutcheon winced as the doctor began to snip the stitches. He was seated by the window and had a good view of the church steeple.

"How'd that church out there burn down?"

"Hmm? Oh . . . fire from a stove. Happened a couple of years ago on a cold night, and there that steeple has stood ever since. The congregation hasn't been able to raise money to replace the building yet. There was no insurance."

"Too bad." He recalled the light he'd seen flicker from the side of the steeple. "Does that steeple have a room in it, by chance?"

"Well, I think it does. Halfway up is a place they

used to store rope and oil and such that they used to keep the bell clean and in good working order. That bell came off an old gunboat from the late war. They took it out after the fire, though."

"A gunboat, huh? Interesting. No chance somebody has taken up lodging in that room, is there?"

Dr. Leedman looked up from his work. "You've seen the light too, eh?"

"Yes. I have."

"I halfway thought it was my imagination," the doctor said, returning to his work and making a final snip. "But apparently not. I'd say some drifter has found himself a free refuge, then. Ah, well. No skin off my nose. It's not my church, and I guess everybody needs a place to stay. Hold still now . . . I've got to do a little tugging."

The actual removal of the stitches hurt more than McCutcheon had expected, but as soon as they were out the itching almost totally vanished.

"Ah. Much better, Doc. Thanks."

"No problem. To put those stitches in yourself you certainly did a yeoman's job. You've got the makings of a physician in you, sir. Ah, well. All done now. Two bits will cover the cost."

McCutcheon paid. "You haven't happened to actually *see* a drifter over at that steeple, have you?"

"Well, I saw a Negro fellow there about dusk one evening. He was walking around toward the back. That doesn't mean he's been up in the tower, though. A lot of people walk through that way, back to the alleyway."

McCutcheon nodded. "Thanks, Doc." He went on his way.

McCutcheon stood on the boardwalk across the street from the ruined church, looking at the steeple. From this angle he could see that there was a small hole in one side about halfway down, maybe damage from a storm or incidental damage done during the fighting of the fire. The hole was located just where he'd seen the light that night as he looked out his hotel window. That verified that the light had been no odd reflection or other fluke. It had shined out from inside, through the hole.

Dr. Leedman said he'd seen a black man nearby. What better place for someone to hide than inside an abandoned steeple? Who would look there?

A black man . . . What if . . . ?

Maybe he wouldn't give up his quest quite yet. He might as well turn over another stone or two, just in case.

McCutcheon returned to his room and strapped on his gun belt. There was a law against wearing guns on the street in this town, as there was in most towns, but McCutcheon's coat was long and he could cover his weaponry for the moment. He wasn't willing to do what he had in mind without protection.

He left the hotel and crossed the street down a few buildings from the burned-out church. He ducked into an alley and went back to a transversing alley at the rear of the row of buildings, and along it cut back toward the church.

He crossed through the blackened rubble of the church house and reached the doorway leading to the steeple stairway. He pulled it open, drew his pistol, and stepped inside.

The stairs creaked despite his best efforts to be quiet, so he put aside any notion of surprising anyone who might be up there. He cocked his pistol and held it before him in both hands so he could aim steadily and fire quickly if violently confronted. But the steeple had an empty feel to it; he did not believe anyone else was present here at the moment.

As the doctor had said, there was a sort of room about halfway up, a kind of wide landing that filled the steeple from wall to wall. There was a coil of rope, an old oil can, a broken wrench.

But what drew McCutcheon's attention was the bedroll spread across the floor, the leather bag, the stack of extra clothing, neatly placed near the foot of the bedroll.

With his heart hammering, McCutcheon walked over, looked at the goods, and shook his head. He glanced up the stairway, then crept up to the belfry to make sure the occupant wasn't hiding up there.

Empty. The man who slept in the bedroll was at the moment away from his makeshift home.

McCutcheon paused a moment to look around from the belfry. From this vantage point he had a clear view of the surrounding countryside. He looked all around the Ozark landscape, looking the longest at a plume of smoke that rose miles away out in the hills. He wondered if someone's house or barn was afire. Another look around and he spotted a second plume rising, some distance from the other, and thicker. Two fires on the same day! Remarkable . . . but it didn't matter to McCutcheon. He had other things to occupy his mind at the moment.

McCutcheon descended to the landing room again. The light was dim, filtering in from above and below and through the single hole in the wall. But he could see well enough to recognize the items he was looking at.

The bedroll, the bag . . . both were familiar. He'd seen them many times before.

A deep sense of regret settled over McCutcheon, and he wished now he'd not left Texas.

He had his answer at last . . . and it was the answer he'd feared. And making it all worse was the awareness that he would have to respond.

McCutcheon reached into his pocket and pulled out a pad of paper and a pencil.

Chapter Twenty-five

The second plume of smoke McCutcheon had seen came from the house of Luther Harper, one of the same Harpers who had gone to set fire to Michael Caywood's barn.

The counterstrike by the Caywoods had apparently been unexpected. Luther Harper and his two sons had put up only a slight resistance before fleeing, with wives, sisters, and children, into the hills. Luke Caywood had stood by, saying nothing but looking like he could keel over sick at any moment.

At one time in his life, Luke had actually enjoyed a sort of friendship with Luther Harper. The pair of them had laid aside old feud animosities and bought some cattle together, running some on Luke's land, some on Luther's. But they had argued—for the life of him Luke couldn't remember over what—and the deal had gone sour. Luke had sold out his share of the cattle to Luther and spent most of the money to finance a very long drunk.

Ben, unlike Luke, had no bad feelings at all about the burning of Luther Harper's place. In Ben's view, not only was it deserved in retaliation for the earlier fire at Michael Caywood's, but also because of the death of his father and the others. His belief that the murders were caused by the Harpers had moved from wild theory to firm and irrevocable conviction.

Ben, his face smudged with ash, ran up to Luke with an expression of almost boyish exuberance. "Ain't it fine, Luke? The Harpers feeling the sting at last!"

"Ben . . . I got to leave. I don't want to be part of this no more."

"Leave?" Ben couldn't seem to grasp it for a few moments. Then his expression darkened. "All right, then leave! Go crawling back! The rest of us will be out here putting an end to the Harpers' running over us roughshod!"

"You've burned a house, Ben. It's enough. An eye for an eye. Let it stop at that."

Ben laughed in contempt. "The blood of my murdered father says it's not enough. The Harpers have more paying to do."

Luke shook his head. "I'm going home. I want no more of this."

Ben swore and waved him off in disgust.

Luke pulled his flask from his pocket and took a long drink, then put it away. He turned to go back to his horse, waiting nearby.

As he turned, Luke saw another man who had been, like himself, only on the fringes of this mad attack. This was Pete Caywood, another distant cousin, and one Luke had not seen for years until this day.

Like the sight of the fire earlier, the sight of Pete Caywood gazing back at him brought a very ugly memory to Luke, the very memory that above all others he had sought to drown through the years in gallons of liquor. He moved his mouth as if to speak to Pete, who had an expression of numb horror on his face, but nothing would come out.

Luke groaned and stumbled to his horse, swung himself into the saddle, and rode away.

Pete Caywood watched him go, then turned and went to his own horse. He mounted much more deftly than had Luke, and rode off after him.

Dusk, the same day

John Mark looked up at Susanna and shook his head.

"He's getting worse," he said. "I should have left for Hulltown long ago."

"He seemed to be improving earlier," Susanna said. "I'm sorry, John Mark. It's my fault. I should have let you go . . . now it's to be dark soon." She paused. "I'll go get Dr. Leedman my-self."

John Mark stood. "No, Miss Susanna. No. You'll not. *I'll* go."

"It's dangerous out there, John Mark. It's my fault for not having gotten the doctor already, and I'll not have you endanger yourself because of my oversight. I'll make the journey."

John Mark was normally not a particularly forceful man, but he came to his feet now and put his face inches from Susanna's.

In the door, Marie and Jeremy glanced at each other, both of them ready to fall apart at any moment, both of them fully useless to the cause at hand, or any other.

"You listen to me, Miss Susanna. I know I'm speaking out of turn, but this time I got to do it. Your father is too sick to speak his own mind, so I'll say what he would say. You ain't going out there in them woods tonight, miss. Not for no reason. You've already come near to being killed out there, and once is enough. I know you see yourself the equal of any man, and God knows you're twice as brave as any man I've ever known. But the point is that your father would want me to protect you. Let me go."

"John Mark, you're too old for this."

"I've made the journey to Hulltown by night and day more times than there are days in your lifetime, Miss Susanna. And I'll do it that many times again. Listen to me, miss. It ain't me he's after. It's the Caywood family. He'll let me pass, if he even sees me at all."

"I can't let you do it, John Mark."

"Miss, you do me the favor of hearing me out. You answer this question honest. If you went out there and something bad happened to you, and Mr. Mack there got better again and found out I let you go, do you think he'd forgive me for it?"

Susanna had to be honest. "No. He wouldn't."

"It's a lot more likely I can make it through safe, Miss Susanna. He's shot you once already. And you've shot at *him*. He'll remember that. Besides, he's a Negro man and so am I. He'll let me pass. I'll have a better chance than you of getting Doc Leedman back here."

Susanna thought about it a few moments. Her father groaned. "All right," she said. "You've persuaded me, John Mark. Take the best horse and arm yourself well. And be careful."

John Mark nodded. "I will, Miss Susanna."

Outside, thunder rumbled. The clouds that had been on the horizon at morning had spread slowly across the sky all day.

Night was coming, and with it, a storm.

Chapter Twenty-six

L uke didn't make it far before he realized someone was coming after him. His first thought was of the mysterious murderer, filling him with panic and the desire to hide.

An old hunter's cabin was in this vicinity, and Luke made for it. He hid his horse in a grove of trees and hunkered down in the cabin with his weapons, ready to defend himself.

But no attack came; he saw no sign of the phantom killer. Out came the flask. An hour, then two, slipped past. The day was moving on, and Luke Caywood was hiding away, wondering what Ben and his little Caywood army were doing now and what the results of it all would be.

He fell asleep, then awakened with the sun westering low. Panic set in all over again; he sensed he wasn't alone.

He wasn't. Seated across from him in the darkening little cabin was Pete Caywood.

"Hello, Luke. Hope I didn't startle you."

"What are you doing here, Pete? I might have shot you."

"You'd never shoot me, Luke."

"How long have you been here?"

"An hour. You've been sleeping."

Luke rubbed his eyes and looked closely at Pete. "Pete . . . are you . . . crying?"

"I am, Luke. Can't help it. Because all these terrible things that are happening are our fault. You and me."

"Our fault? What are you talking about?"

"You know what I'm talking about. Think back, Luke. Think back to what you and me both have tried not to remember for so many years. The barn, the fire . . ."

"Shut up, Pete! Don't talk about that! We both vowed years ago that nothing more ever would be said about that night."

"It has to be said now. Because of all that's happening."

"No," Luke said, turning his head. "I won't hear this. I won't listen."

"You have to listen."

Outside, the wind howled as the storm moved in.

Old Barnabas lived in a small two-room house on the side of Hullville where most of the limited black populace of the town resided.

He'd built the little porch on the front of the

house with his own hands a quarter of a century earlier. By now, it, like its builder, was beginning to sag a bit, but it would be years before it fell.

The wind was whipping around his house, threatening to blow the hat from his head. One hand held his hat on, the other dug deep in his pocket.

He'd been thinking hard ever since that inquisitive young fellow had showed up at the shop earlier, and things that had been murky and buried in the back swamps of his mind had begun to emerge.

He knew now that, coming storm or not, he had to go visit Jim McCutcheon at the hotel and tell him what he had remembered.

Pulling his coat tight around him and pushing his hat down harder on his gray head, Old Barnabas walked up the street toward the Hulltown Hotel.

The rain began to patter down as he reached the hotel. He took off his hat, shook the rain from it, and put it back on his head, noticing that his hand was trembling as he did it. This business had him rather nervous.

Barnabas went to the desk and inquired about which room was occupied by Jim McCutcheon. He trudged up the stairs, reached the door, hesitated, then knocked.

He stepped back with a gasp when Jim McCutcheon yanked the door open and greeted him with an upraised pistol. McCutcheon's eyes widened, and he lowered the pistol right away.

"Barnabas! I'm sorry . . . I thought you were someone else."

Barnabas tried to answer, realized he was involuntarily holding his breath, and gasped out loudly a couple of times. "Pardon me . . . for surprising you so, sir."

"Come in, Barnabas. I truly am sorry. Come in and sit down. Let me get you some water. I'm so very sorry about the pistol."

"I will sit down, sir. I've got something to tell you." Barnabas was so breathless he could hardly speak.

"Have you remembered something?" McCutcheon was pouring a glass of clean water from the pitcher on his washstand.

"I have, sir," Barnabas said, accepting the glass in two cupped and trembling hands. He took a long swallow, water trickling out of both corners of his mouth. He gave the glass back to McCutcheon and swiped his mouth with the back of his hand.

"I think I know who it is out there killing people in the woods," Barnabas said.

The departure of Luke had bothered Ben a little more than he wanted to admit. Up until that point he had been operating in a kind of mad passion fueled by the company of other men equally inflamed with anger. The riding to the Harper place, the torching of it, the exchange of gunfire with the fleeing occupants . . . Ben had never felt such a boiling in his blood as he did when those events were taking place.

Luke's departure had splashed some cold water on his inner fire and made him question what he and the others were doing. Might there be a price to pay later on for this violent sweep? Could they really get by with taking the law into their own hands like this? He hadn't thought much beyond the immediate moment.

It appeared, though, that no one else was thinking beyond the moment, either. Michael Caywood had become the unofficial leader of this effort, his burning of one Harper farmstead seemingly only adding to his desire to do the same thing again, bigger and hotter than before. Ben may have started this ball rolling, but its momentum had been picked up by others.

Ben spurred his horse and rode up near Michael. "Where exactly are we going now?" he asked.

"Merrill Harper's spread, just ahead in the hollow. Merrill was another one of the Harpers who burned my house. Now we'll see how he likes getting the same."

"It's getting ready to storm," Ben said. "It'll be hard to burn a house in the rain, won't it?"

"With some coal oil on it, it'll burn just fine. You wait and see. Don't get weak-kneed on me, Ben. You're the one who inspired all this."

"Yes . . . but maybe we're moving too fast, Michael. We've got to plan our actions. The Harpers may be expecting something like this now. They may be waiting for us."

"No, Ben, no. Moving fast is the key. Merrill Harper won't be expecting this tonight. Nobody will. Two Harper burnings in one night? Uh-uh. Nobody will be looking for that."

Ben wasn't so sure. This group, which had grown by the addition of several other bloodthirsty Caywoods within the last hour, had left a very noticeable calling card in the burning of Luther Harper's house, and Merrill Harper's was the next nearest Harper residence. It would be the obvious place the Harpers would expect this group to strike next.

Rain began to fall, and lightning flared across the sky, filling the narrow hollow before them with light.

The storm heightened Ben's trepidation. "Michael, don't do this. Pull back. This isn't the time."

Michael glared at him through the rain and darkness. "It's the *only* time, Ben. They'll never expect us in this storm."

"It's just a feeling I've got."

"Forget about it . . . and shut up. There's no more time for talk."

They went on, but Ben let himself fall back toward the rear. The storm rose, drenching all of them, making it difficult for them to progress. The lightning had Ben's horse badly spooked and he struggled to keep control of the animal.

He thought about dropping back completely, letting the night swallow him, and riding back home. The temptation was strong, but if he did that, his absence would be noticed eventually, and concerns would rise about what had happened to him. A search for him might put the searchers in danger from lurking Harpers. So he rode on.

The lightning suddenly revealed their target: a board-and-batten farmhouse, surrounded by outbuildings, farther down in the narrow hollow. The line of horsemen advanced, then gathered. Torches fired with coal oil were lit, and at a signal from Michael, the riders advanced at full gallop.

Ben was with them, torch in hand and heart in throat. Down the narrow hollow they rode, racing toward the house. Ben wondered how many were inside . . . if there were women and children.

He didn't want to do this. The fire that had so inflamed him before had almost fully died away.

They were within a hundred yards of the

house when the shooting began. Gunfire erupted from both sides of the hollow. Ben heard screams, whinnies, saw horses rear and riders fall, torches arcing to the ground and sizzling in the running rainwater . . .

"Ambush!" someone yelled. "*Ambush!*"

Ben wheeled his panicking horse, tossing his torch aside and thinking now only of escape. But the horse was uncooperative, pitching about, almost throwing him.

He got it under control as carnage continued around him, powder flares and gunshots filling the hollow with terror and confusion. Ben wanted to scream, to pray, to curse. Michael Caywood had been wrong: The Harpers had not been surprised at all by this second excursion, but *expecting* it, awaiting it, with groves and gullies full of armed and ambushing Harpers, as intent on their own vengeance as the Caywoods had been on theirs . . .

Ben bent low in the saddle, racing hard, putting the carnage behind him . . .

When a bullet slapped into his side it was like being stabbed with a poker fired red hot. Ben cried out and fell headlong from the saddle, facedown in the mud. His horse ran on without him.

He groaned, tried to push himself up, but was too weak to make it all the way. His body throbbed with pain. He twisted his head and saw others fleeing the valley, coming at him, three horses bearing down upon him . . .

His final scream was crushed into silence beneath a flurry of pounding hooves.

Chapter Twenty-seven

Luke Caywood, seated on the ground in the crumbling little hunter's cabin, shook his head in a violent rejection of what Pete Caywood had just finished spelling out to him.

"No," he said. "No. I won't believe it. I will *not* believe it, will *not* accept it."

Pete Caywood's face was hidden by the darkness, though the occasional flash of lightning would reveal half of it.

"It's true, Luke. This is our fault. You and me. We thought we could turn our heads and make what we did go away, but the world don't work that way. Our sin has found us out."

Luke closed his eyes and drank again from his flask. It was almost empty now. "I don't remember much about that night."

"Don't lie to me, Luke. We both remember every bit of it. We always will."

"It wasn't our fault! It was Eli Harper who had her in that barn! We didn't know!"

"You're right. It wasn't just our sin. It was us

and Eli together. Caywood and Harper. Now both families are being punished. That's how I figured it out . . . the name Nora, and the killing of both Harpers and Caywoods."

Luke had nothing to say. He finished his liquor with hands shaking like leaves in the wind.

Off in the distance, in the direction from which Luke and Pete Caywood had come, gunfire erupted. A lot of it, all at once, like a battle suddenly launched. It went on far too long.

Luke lowered his head, not wanting to hear it.

"Dear God!" Pete Caywood sobbed suddenly. "Dear God, it sounds like an ambush!"

"No, Pete. Just shut up!"

"Our fault, Luke. Our fault. Look at us, both of us . . . no account at all, no good to anybody . . . hiding our secrets, drinking our whiskey . . . and now people are dying because of what we done."

"I don't want to hear you, Pete!"

Pete reached down and brought up something in his hand. Luke looked but could not tell what it was.

"Shall I go first, or you?"

"What do you mean?"

"Our sins have found us out. I can't go on once the truth is known by everybody."

"You're scaring me, Pete. What are you talking about?"

"I'll go first," Pete said, crying harder. "When I'm done, you can do it after me."

"Do what, Pete?" Luke was wanting to cry himself now, and he wasn't sure why.

The explosion of the pistol was terribly loud. In the flash of it, for less than a second, Luke saw Pete's face, mouth open, pistol thrust into it and pointing up.

Luke screamed as Pete fell to one side, instantly dead, the top of his head gone. Luke was still screaming as he fetched his horse, mounted, and rode as hard as he could through the storm toward Mack's house miles away.

John Mark had never liked to admit that he was not a young man anymore, but tonight, riding pell-mell through the storm toward Hulltown, he couldn't deny it. This adventurous ride would have been exhilarating to him at one time in his life, but tonight he was terrified, cold, afraid of failure. Even though it was the horse, not he, who was putting forth the true exertion, he was out of breath and tiring rapidly, just from riding.

But he had to keep going, all the way to Hulltown, even if it killed his horse, or him. John Mark was deeply worried about Mack, afraid he would die. The lung illness that had Mack in its grip had never squeezed him so tightly as it had today. John Mark wondered if they had waited too long to go fetch the doctor, and cursed himself for his overconfidence in his own medical abilities. This was one time he'd not been able to bring down a fever like he usually could.

He prayed hard that Mack Caywood would keep hanging on until Dr. Leedman could be brought to him.

John Mark never saw what spooked his horse. Suddenly, though, the animal whinnied and reared high. John Mark struggled to hold on, but lost his grip and tumbled out of the saddle onto the rain-soaked ground. The layer of damp leaves was even softer than usual because of the heavy rain, and no doubt spared him from worse injury than he might have received from a hard landing. But his left foot had hung up a moment in the stirrup as he fell, twisting his ankle badly. Fortunately, his foot pulled free just in time to keep his horse from dragging him as it ran on down the forest road.

Groaning, John Mark pushed himself up to a seated posture and winced at the pain stabbing through his ankle. What a time for such an accident! He wasn't sure he could catch his horse again even if he wasn't injured. Doing so with a twisted ankle, in the midst of storm and darkness like this, would be all the more of a challenge.

He managed to pull himself up using a sapling for support. His ankle proved capable of bearing a little weight, but he wanted to yell every time he stepped with it.

The lightning revealed his horse up ahead. It had stopped running, but looked ready to bolt again. John Mark wished he'd selected a different horse. This one was the fastest in the entire Caywood remuda, but also more prone to skittishness. Because the present circumstances had called for speed, however, it had seemed worth the risk to choose the fastest horse.

John Mark took a step and fell, but by luck put his hand down on a large stick, which he used to push himself up again. Using the stick like a rough cane, he advanced again toward the horse—then in a rush ducked into a nearby grove of trees when the lightning revealed something unexpected and chilling.

A man was moving through the woods on foot. He was armed and had something thrust into his belt that was either a short sword or very long knife. Though it was hard to be sure, it appeared that the man was black.

John Mark knew he'd just run across the killer in the hills.

He prayed that he'd not been seen in turn. He'd seen the man in profile, meaning the man might not have seen him unless John Mark's movement had caught the corner of his vision. It took several moments for lightning to flash again, but when it did, the man was gone.

John Mark still dared not move. The man might be hiding, waiting for him to emerge.

A glance down the road revealed that his horse was still there. Either the forest lurker had not seen the horse or was letting it serve as bait to draw John Mark out.

For ten minutes John Mark remained where he was, then decided to risk moving. He got up and hobbled out with his stick, heading for his horse, which had moved a little farther down the narrow road.

No one shot at him, accosted him, or otherwise reacted to his reappearance. Apparently the killer really had not seen him or his horse.

John Mark got into the saddle with some difficulty and began to ride again toward Hulltown.

A part of him wanted to return to the Caywood house, just in case that killer went there—with John Mark, Luke, and Ben all absent, and Mack in no condition to put up a defense. But John Mark had an assignment to complete, and besides, the killer had never struck anyone except lone woodland travelers. There was no reason he'd be likely to change his mode of operation tonight.

Chapter Twenty-eight

Luke Caywood was still in tears when he reached the edge of Mack's ranch. He pulled his weary, soaked horse to a halt and slumped out of the saddle, barely able to walk.

He'd gone over an emotional edge, suffered a full-fledged breakdown. The horror of seeing Pete blow his brains out like that, the sick suspicion that Ben and the others had been ambushed on their way to burn down another Harper house, and the guilt of thinking that something he and Pete had done years ago was the cause of all the murders of late, combined to ruin him. He wanted only to hide and get drunk and never be sober, or seen, again.

He didn't stable his horse, just let it trail off on its own, still saddled. It made for the stable while Luke staggered toward the barn.

Inside, he entered a back stall and collapsed, weeping. After a few minutes he got up and went to an empty storage bin, and out of the bit of dried hay that filled its bottom, pulled a bottle.

It was one of many bottles he kept hidden all around the grounds, just for convenience.

Luke pulled the cork out and turned the bottle up. He was determined to drink until he could drink no more, and if he was lucky, he would never wake up again.

Old Barnabas, a little calmer and drier now, looked at McCutcheon, who sat in a chair beside the table lamp, the warm glow spilling across the left side of his face.

"It was you mentioning the name 'Jake' that got me to thinking back and finally remembering," Barnabas said. "I told you about the woman I talked to one day on the road, the Negro woman named Nora."

"Yes . . . but you weren't sure her name really was Nora."

"I'm sure now. I remember it clear now. The more I've thunk back today, the clearer it all became. She was Nora . . . and the day she talked to me, all crying and weeping and talking about how bad her man treated her, she mentioned the name of Jake. I don't recall no last name, just Jake. She said that he was her brother, I think, and that if he was there, he'd never stand for her husband beating on her."

McCutcheon struggled not to tremble. This was the most exact piece of news yet to emerge about Jake's missing sister. The Nora that Old

Barnabas had talked to could surely be no one else.

But there was tragedy in this news as well. "Earlier today, you said that the woman you spoke to died in a fire."

"Yes."

"And it struck me that you didn't want to speak about it."

"I didn't, sir. But I've been studying on it today, and decided that I will speak about it. I think you should hear the truth . . . and see that maybe we've stumbled over the answer to why there's somebody out in the hills murdering Harpers and Caywoods."

"Tell me all you can."

Old Barnabas resettled himself and took a deep breath. "Back in those days, the Harper and Caywood feud was going stronger than it has in recent years. There was true fighting out in these hills, men killing one another and the law usually never knowing about it. It wouldn't have mattered much, anyway. Between the Caywoods and Harpers, it's always just been the law of the feud, and nobody's ever been able to change it.

"Luke Caywood, the brother of Mack, and his cousin Pete Caywood, were drinking one day in a barroom out in one of the little mountain communities in this county, when in comes Eli Harper. One of the worst of the Harper clan. He was a man with a reputation with the women, and he bragged on it a lot, but the truth was that not all the women he was with were with him by choice. He'd force them, you see."

"He was a rapist," McCutcheon said forthrightly.

"Yes, sir, he was. More than one time. But he was mean as a snake and had all the Harpers behind him, and nobody dared to touch him.

"That day in that barroom, Eli had words with Luke and Pete Caywood, and it come to blows. Somebody busted up the fight, and Eli saw the better part of good sense and fled. But the two Caywoods had more liquor than common sense in them at that point, and they took off after him, with Eli not knowing.

"To make a long story short, it all wound up with Eli in a barn loft, and the two Caywoods trying to sneak up on him. But he caught them at it and fired some shots. They tried to get at him but couldn't, and they got the notion of setting the barn afire to drive him out. It was a Harper barn, so they had no second thoughts about burning it.

"They set that barn to burning, but it didn't drive Eli out. Instead he got caught and burned alive, along with some cattle and horses. If you ask me, the cattle and horses was the greater loss. But still, there was a man dead, and the two Caywood cousins decided to keep mum about it all to make sure they never got in trouble for it.

"Well, a day or two later, Nora's husband comes around asking where his wife, Nora, might have got to. He couldn't find her nowhere. In the meantime, they'd found the burned-up corpse of Eli Harper in that barn rubble, and something else, too: a second corpse, smaller than Eli's but just as badly burned. It appeared to be a woman's corpse, and there was a melted bit of bracelet about what was left of her wrist that verified it. By and by folks began to put two and two together, and they showed the bracelet to this Negro fellow, and he wails out that it is his wife's bracelet, sure as anything. Then, no more than two days later, this fellow gets himself arrested for some thievery he'd been involved in, and hauled off for a long stretch of time in jail. That was the last anybody I know of seen of him.

"The official version of it all was that the fire had started for reasons unknown, and that Eli Harper had the misfortune of getting caught in it while he was doing things he shouldn't with the wife of a Negro man. But the truth was, Luke and Pete Caywood had started that fire. They killed Eli Harper and the Nora woman as sure as if they'd shot them. But all in all, nobody ever knew."

A peel of thunder rolled over the town. The storm was still going, but it was beginning to weaken a little. McCutcheon said, "If nobody's ever talked, then how do *you* know about it?"

"There was another person in that barn, that's how I know. A ragged little mulatto boy who used to live around here in sheds and barns and such, begging his living. He was in that barn when Eli brought the woman in. He never got a good look at them, but being a boy, he was interested in what Eli and that woman was doing, and listened. But when Luke and Pete showed up with that flame, he skedaddled out of there. They never seen him at all."

"He told you about this?"

"Yes."

"But you never told the law."

"I didn't want to get Mr. Luke in trouble, sir. His family's been mighty good to my brother. When you're a man of color living amongst people who don't always think highly of your kind, you learn real fast that the best thing for you to do most of the time is keep your lip buttoned up tight. That's what I done . . . until tonight."

McCutcheon stared off into the corner. "So Jake has spent all these years looking for his sister, and she's been dead all that time. I wonder . . . maybe Jake learned the truth about what happened. Maybe he talked to that same mulatto who hid in the barn, or to somebody else that the mulatto had told the story to. And maybe it drove Jake over the edge with grief, and made him decide to avenge himself on the Caywoods for setting the fire that killed his sister."

"It could be, sir."

"But why would he also kill Harpers?"

"Remember what I told you about Eli Harper, sir. He forced himself on women. Just because Nora was in that barn with him don't mean she was there because she wanted to be. He raped her, sir, just to say it right out."

McCutcheon nodded. "So the Harpers get blame, too. Jake kills Caywoods because of the fire, and Harpers because of the rape."

"Might be, sir. It might be."

McCutcheon had nothing more to say. This was all too stunning.

Old Barnabas let out a sudden gasp, and came clumsily to his feet, backing away and staring at the room's back window.

McCutcheon looked and came to his feet as well.

On the other side of the window, looking back inside with rain dripping from his hat and soaking his clothing, was Jake Penn.

Chapter Twenty-nine

For a couple of moments, McCutcheon was stricken by the same kind of fear he would have felt had he seen an authentic ghost.

The window was on the second story, yet Penn was outside it as if it were ground level and he had his feet planted on the earth. McCutcheon was overwhelmed with the absurd notion that Penn was somehow floating up, looking through the window like a bobbing phantom. The person who had been McCutcheon's closest friend and partner had now become a supernatural, evil entity in McCutcheon's mind.

The misperception about floating didn't last for long. McCutcheon quickly recalled that there was a narrow, railed porch that extended the length of the building on the rear. It was on the top of this porch that Penn was standing.

McCutcheon drew his pistol, went to the window, and slid it up. He leveled his pistol on Penn and said, "Come in . . . slow."

Penn gaped at him. "Jim, what the devil are you doing? It's me, Jake Penn!"

"I know who you are, Jake. It's what you've become that I'm not sure about, and I've got a bullet furrow through my side that tells me to be mighty careful about you now."

Penn looked perplexed and hurt. He stared uncomprehendingly at McCutcheon as he carefully came inside, dripping water all over.

"Jim, I don't understand why you're giving me this kind of reception." He glanced over at Barnabas, who was looking at Penn as if he was the devil incarnated. "Who is this gentleman?"

McCutcheon ignored the question. "Unhitch your gun belt, Penn, and let it drop to the floor, really slow. Then scoot it toward me with your foot. And get that little hideout pistol out of your boot and kick it out of the way, too." It felt quite strange to be ordering his old partner around in such a hostile way. Then again, that bullet furrowing through his side had felt a bit strange, too.

Penn complied, frowning now. "Why are you doing this, Jim?"

"Why does anybody do anything, Jake? Why do people hide out in old church towers like rats in a hole? Why do people shoot at women in the woods, and plow a bullet through the side of an old friend?"

Penn was utterly bewildered. "Jim, what are you talking about?"

McCutcheon was embarrassed by how visibly his gun was shaking. "You shot me the other night, Penn. Out in the woods while you were in the midst of a gun battle with Susanna Caywood."

Penn gaped, then laughed. "*Shot* you? I never shot you or anybody else, Jim! I don't even know who Susanna Caywood is."

"Why are you here, Jake?"

"Because I found a note from my old partner, telling me where I could find him and asking me to come. I found it right where you'd left it over yonder in my room in the belfry. I rejoiced to find that note, Jim. I had no idea you were in this town until I found it."

"You expect me to believe that? Are you saying it wasn't you who put a bullet through me out in the woods?"

"It wasn't me. For God's sake, Jim, it's *me*! It's Jake! What do you think? That I'd ever shoot you, for any reason?"

McCutcheon lowered the gun a little. "But it happened, Jake. I saw you do it. I felt the bullet."

"Whoever it was, it wasn't me. Maybe somebody that looked like me. Did you get a clear look?"

"As clear a look as you can in the span of a lightning flash."

"Jim, whoever you saw might look like me, but I swear before God it wasn't. Think about it, Jim. I'm Jake. I'm your partner. I don't have gunfights with women or shoot my old friends."

McCutcheon lowered the gun fully. "I know you don't. I'm sorry, Jake. It wasn't you."

Penn smiled. "Glad you've reached that conclusion." He glanced at Barnabas. "Who's your friend here?"

"This is Barnabas. Barnabas, meet Jake Penn."

The old man nodded, looking a little suspicious and perplexed by all of this.

"How bad shot were you, Jim?" Penn asked.

McCutcheon pulled up his shirt and revealed the pink and still-healing flesh. "Nothing serious. Barnabas' brother, John Mark, stitched me up good. He works for Mack Caywood, the father of the Susanna Caywood I mentioned."

"Caywood is a name of note from these parts lately," Penn said. "I hear there's been some trouble for that family recently."

McCutcheon played a hunch. "Just what drew you to this county, Penn?"

Penn reached under his soggy coat and pulled out a folded piece of newspaper, which he handed to McCutcheon. It was a clipping of the same story that McCutcheon had read that night on his porch back in Texas.

"I should have known," he said, handing it back to Penn. "I should have realized that if you saw that story, it would raise for you the same questions it did for me . . . well, not *exactly* the same questions."

Penn thought it over a moment. "Jim, you wondered if it was me doing those killings? Because the killer is a Negro, and because of the reference to Nora in the notes he leaves?"

"Jake, it makes me feel ashamed to admit it now. I know you couldn't have done such things . . . but I had to prove it to myself. So I came to Arkansas, and promptly got shot by somebody who appeared to be you. Then I find a hidden room in a church steeple that's got your bedroll and goods in it . . . what was I supposed to think? And if you're not the one, why have you been hiding out in a burned-out church?"

"Under the circumstances, it isn't wise for a black man of my age to be showing himself openly. There's a good likelihood of getting strung up by a mob of angry Caywoods."

"Or Harpers," McCutcheon threw in. "That's a family that feuds with the Caywoods, and some of them have been murdered, too."

"Same notes about Nora?"

"Yes."

"So somebody is taking out on two Ozark families something to do with a woman named Nora . . ."

"Penn, you and me need to talk. I've found some answers to some old questions . . . found

them this very night, thanks to Old Barnabas. I
know some of what became of Nora, Penn."

He gazed at McCutcheon. "She's dead, ain't
she?"

"Yes, Jake. I'm sorry."

Penn drew in his breath very slowly, then
pursed his lips and nodded. "A part of me has always wondered if maybe that's what I'd find at
the end." He looked away, blinking a few times,
drawing in a couple of more ragged breaths.
"How long has it been?"

"Many years."

"A natural death?"

McCutcheon felt ill. How can you tell a man
that the sister he spent years searching for died
in flames after being raped and abused by an evil
man? "Penn, the story is a sad one. There are
parts of it I'm loath to tell you."

"Tell me. I'd rather know than not."

Briefly, McCutcheon outlined what Barnabas
had told him. He could see that it jolted Penn to
hear it, but Penn held up well. "Dear God," was
all he whispered at the end.

"I'm sorry to have to tell you such a thing,
Jake. It grieves me."

"The truth is the truth. A man has to face it
sometime." Penn swallowed hard. "I'll tell you,
and it's a terrible thing to say, but it almost puts
me in some sympathy with whoever is doing
those murders. I can understand hating a family

who raped your wife, and another family who set a fire that burned her to death."

"There's only one problem with that, Jake: It wasn't a family who raped Nora. It was one man. And it wasn't an entire family who set that barn afire, but two cousins who didn't even know she was in the barn at all."

"I know. I know."

"But the question remains, Penn: If it isn't you who is avenging Nora, then who is it?"

"It's clear to me who it is," Penn said.

"I think I know, too," Barnabas cut in. "I think maybe her sorry old husband has come back to kill all the Caywoods and Harpers he can, until he gets killed himself."

Chapter Thirty

"Pardon me, but that doesn't make a lot of sense," McCutcheon said. "If he was the kind of man who beat her, then why would he want to avenge her?"

"I've known men of that sort in my time," Penn said. "To them a woman is something you possess, something you control and dominate. That's their sorry version of 'love.' When a man like that sees others take advantage of his woman, or even hurt her, he sees something that belongs to him being took advantage of or hurt. He sees it as an insult to him as the possessor of that woman. So he lashes out." Penn turned to Barnabas. "I agree with you, sir. It's almost certainly Nora's husband who has come back."

"We never really knew for sure that Nora was married until now," McCutcheon observed.

"Actually, Jim, I did know. Since you and I parted ways I've picked up a lot of trails and learned a lot of things. Having money enabled me to advertise for information and pay informants and so on, and I was able to learn that Nora had married a man named Nicholas Click—"

Old Barnabas nodded broadly. "Yes, that's the name! I remember it now! Nicholas Click . . . that was Nora's husband."

Penn picked up right where Barnabas had cut in: "—and lived briefly with him in Alabama, then Texas, then Arkansas. But the trail grew cold after that. I could find nothing more of Nora at all, and nothing definite about Click except that he spent several years in prison for being part of a big ring of thieves. By then Nora had faded out of the picture, and I couldn't find out why. I feared she might have died. You can imagine, Jim, how quick I was to travel here once I saw that newspaper article. A black man killing to avenge a woman named Nora right in the very region that my Nora lived . . . I knew there had to be a connection. And when I saw the part about vengeance, I had to assume the worst, that Nora was probably dead."

"I wish she wasn't."

Penn shivered. "I've soaked myself to the skin coming up to see you, Jim. But I'm glad to see you, even if you do bear such sad news."

"You have an odd way of entering hotel rooms, Jake. I never had a visitor come through my window before."

"Like I said, a black man of my age and description has to keep his profile low in these parts just now, unless he doesn't mind being hung as a murderer, probably with no trial. I've had to keep myself completely hidden. That belfry was just the place."

"Not entirely. You were seen by at least one man, Jake. The doctor whose office is down the row a couple of buildings saw a black man near the steeple. Probably you."

"Probably. Thank God he didn't report me. But how did you know I was there?"

McCutcheon described what had happened.

Penn said, "Jim, we've got a lot of catching up to do. What have you gone and done with yourself since we parted ways, Jim?"

"Gotten engaged to be married."

That one interested Penn for sure. A long overdue conversation began between Penn and McCutcheon, with Barnabas sitting in just as a listener. Despite the presence of a third party, McCutcheon spoke freely, confessing his doubts about his wedding plans, even the racism of Emily's father and—he had to admit—Emily herself.

Barnabas eventually grew somewhat bored with the conversation, most of which meant nothing to him. He rose and went to the window, looking out at the storm as it dwindled to a steady shower.

"Mr. McCutcheon," he said as he looked out

onto the street. "I believe I see my brother out here."

"What? You mean John Mark?"

"The only brother I got, sir. Please come and look . . . I think he's hurt."

McCutcheon and Penn went to the window. Below, John Mark had just dismounted from his horse and was hobbling noticeably toward a building slightly up the street and on the same side of it as the hotel.

"He's going to the doctor's office," McCutcheon said. "Why would he ride all the way from the Caywood ranch in a storm? Barnabas, you stay here. Penn and I will go see what's wrong."

John Mark was in quite an overwrought state when McCutcheon reached him. His heaving horse was exhausted almost to the point of ruination.

"Mr. McCutcheon, sir! I've come here to fetch the doctor for Mr. Mack, but he's not here . . ."

"Calm down, John Mark. Tell me what's wrong with Mack."

John Mark caught sight of Penn and backed away two steps. "Who is he?"

"Not who you think. He's an old friend of mine named Jake Penn. You can trust him. Tell me what's wrong with Mack."

"He's mighty sick, mighty sick. Terrible fever, and nothing I could do would bring it down."

Penn had walked to the doctor's door and came back with a note in hand. "This says the doctor has gone to deliver a baby," he said. "You're not going to be able to find him, it appears."

"Then I'm going back," John Mark said. "I got to go back and try some more to get his fever down."

"No, John Mark," McCutcheon said. "You're injured and exhausted. You go up to my room. Your brother is already there. You get some rest. Penn and I will go back to the Caywood house and see what we can do. Penn's a right good rough-and-ready physician himself."

"Then please hurry, because he's mighty sick, and there's nobody there except Miss Susanna and Miss Marie and young Jeremy."

"Where's Ben and Luke?"

"I don't know for certain, but I think they went off to fight Harpers. They haven't come back, and I'm afraid something's wrong with them, too."

"How long a ride is it?" Penn asked.

McCutcheon made a mental estimate. "If we push our horses, we can make it well before dawn."

"One problem," Penn said. "I've got no horse just now. I had no place to keep it and paid a rancher at the edge of the valley to take care of it a spell."

"Then you're going to be a horse thief after all," McCutcheon said. "We'll get my horse out of the livery and borrow one for you. We'll make it right later."

"Be careful," John Mark said. "I seen him. I seen the killer. And if nobody gets back there soon, I know good and well what Miss Susanna will do. She'll head out her own self, all alone, thinking that something has happened to me. She'll be out there all alone, with that murderer."

"We will be very careful, and we'll move fast," McCutcheon said. "Come on. Let me help you up to my room. Then Penn and I will be on our way."

Chapter Thirty-one

Joe Tifton had not remained in Hulltown more than a day before returning to again haunt the woods around the Caywood ranch, protecting his beloved Deborah.

He'd remained outdoors most of that time, but the storm that had struck tonight had driven him toward the barn, where he'd holed up in the loft and fallen asleep in a mound of hay while listening to the thunder roll. Joe Tifton had been like that since boyhood: He always slept best during storms.

Now that the storm was abating, he woke. Sitting up, he looked around the dark stall . . . and heard something unexpected below.

Somebody was moving around down there, rustling hay about, bumping the sides of the stalls, even singing softly in a low, sad, drunken-sounding voice. He heard the faint clink of a bottle against a tooth.

Moving slowly, Joe snaked out along the loft until he could see over the edge. It was terribly dark, but he could just make out the form of a man in the stall below him. When he heard the voice, half singing and half moaning, he knew who it was.

"Luke Caywood!" he said in a loud whisper. "Luke, is that you?"

The man below started badly at the sound of Joe's voice, almost dropping the bottle. "Lord! Who's that? Who's up there?"

"Don't worry, Luke, it's not the murderer. It's just me, Joe Tifton."

"Joe . . . I thought you'd been told to go away!"

"Mack can tell me to go away all he wants. It don't matter. As long as Deborah is here and there's a killer on the loose out there, I'll be in the vicinity, like it or not."

Luke, very drunk, began to cry and groan. "It's my fault, Joe. Did you know that? All these murders are my fault."

Joe knew Luke for the drunk he was and never paid much heed to the things he said, even when sober. "I don't think so, Luke. I think it's the killer's fault. I'm coming down there—don't be startled."

Joe climbed down the loft ladder and went to the door of the stall where Luke had ensconced himself.

"Why are you lying around in here?" he asked. "Why don't you just go to the house?"

"I don't deserve to be there, not among the decent folks . . . it's my fault, Joe. If not for me and poor old Pete, none of this would be happening. Poor old Pete!" Luke stuck his finger into his mouth and made a motion as if firing a pistol. "Poor old Pete!"

Joe looked sadly at the pitiful figure and privately vowed never to become a victim of liquor.

"Come on, Luke. Let's get you to the porch. The rain's let up a little. You can stay there a minute while I hide again, then go in."

"You're a good boy, Joe. I don't deserve such friendship. Poor old Pete!" He repeated the pistol-shooting gesture and Joe wondered if the man had drunken himself past the point of sanity.

Joe helped Luke get up. "Don't you tell Mack that I'm out here," he said.

"Mum's the word, Joe. Mum's the word for my good friend Joe Tifton!"

"How much have you had to drink today, Luke?"

"Not enough, Joe. I still remember that it's all my fault. Ben's dead, you know."

"What?"

"They ambushed them. The Harpers did. I heard it all with my own ears. Blam! Blam! Blam! Just like that."

"How do you know Ben is dead? Did you see it?"

"No. I heard it, though."

Joe again discounted Luke's babble. The man was lost in an unstable world all his own.

"I'll bet Ben is fine. I bet he's up there sleeping in his room. Come on. Let's get you to the house."

But at the door of the barn, Joe pulled back suddenly and shoved Luke over into the darkest shadows.

"Why'd you push me, Joe?"

Joe Tifton lifted a hand for silence and kept peering out. After a few moments he said, "Luke, you stay put where you are. Don't come out until I come back for you. And don't make any noise. Stay hidden."

"What's happening, Joe?"

"I just saw something, that's all. I'll go investigate it. You lay low."

"I will. I will. You be careful."

Joe crept out of the barn and headed toward the woodshed, using it and a few of the yard trees as cover to keep himself hidden from the dark figure he'd just seen moving across the yard, toward the house.

The man had been alone, and though the night made it hard to tell, Joe thought he was a black fellow.

The rain had completely stopped by the time Penn and McCutcheon reached the Caywood house. Along the way, as best as he could do while riding breakneck through the dark woods, McCutcheon had tried to fill Penn in on the people in the Caywood family. He told Penn that he loved Susanna Caywood and found as he said it that there was no sense of having said more than the simple truth.

He did love Susanna, and he would not marry Emily Pike. Even if Susanna wouldn't have him he wouldn't marry Emily, because a man shouldn't marry a woman he doesn't love.

They dismounted among the trees on the northeast side of the house.

"Looks peaceful enough," Penn observed.

"Look . . . lights burning inside the house at this hour. Mack must still be awful sick if they're staying up."

"Why don't you go knock on the door. They know you. You can tell them who I am and maybe they'll let me in, too."

"All right."

McCutcheon crossed the yard and went to the door. Gently he rapped on it, then immediately called out in a moderated voice: "Susanna! Marie! Anybody . . . it's Jim McCutcheon."

No answer came back. That seemed odd. Clearly someone was at home.

He rapped harder. Still no answer.

McCutcheon peered through the window in the door.

"Dear Lord!" he said in a sharp whisper. Then, loudly, he yelled, "Penn! Penn, come here!"

McCutcheon hammered the door open even before Penn got to him.

Joe Tifton lay on the floor before the fireplace, covered in blood, the floor around him slick with blood, the poker of the fireplace stained with blood. It had been used to bludgeon him severely, and McCutcheon could tell even as he knelt at Joe's side that the young man was not long for the world.

"Joe, who did this to you?"

Joe tried to talk, but nothing emerged from his lips but crimson bubbles.

"Where are the others, Joe? Where?"

Joe turned his eyes to one side and died.

McCutcheon was heartsick. He'd hardly known Joe, but had liked him very much. How many young men would spend long nights alone in cold woods, keeping watch for a killer just to be sure the girl he loved was safe? Joe Tifton was a hero, in McCutcheon's estimation, and to see him die in this way infuriated him.

Penn, with pistol in hand, was already edging into the next room.

"Nobody here," he said.

"I'm going to find Mack, and Susanna," McCutcheon said. He drew his pistol and headed through the house, carefully, toward Mack's room.

Mack was there, lying on his back. On his chest was a note reading VENGEANCE FOR NORA. McCutcheon ripped it away and threw it on the floor. Beneath it was blood.

"Stabbed . . ." McCutcheon murmured.

To his surprise, Mack's eyes fluttered. He looked at McCutcheon.

"My . . . girls . . . Jeremy . . ."

"Where are they, Mack?"

"Ran . . . away . . ."

"Mack, I want to help you."

"Too late for me . . . Go find my girls . . . and Jeremy . . ."

His eyes closed.

Chapter Thirty-two

Penn was in the door behind McCutcheon. "No one else in the house."

McCutcheon lifted his hand. "Listen!"

"It's coming from the barn," Penn said. "Sounds like someone fighting, maybe . . . yelling . . ."

They left the house together, racing out toward the barn.

Luke Caywood was there, locked in battle with a strongly built black man, about Penn's size and age. As Penn saw him, it was easy to understand how McCutcheon could have mistaken this fellow for him, especially in the confusion of a gun battle and lightning storm.

As old and drunk as he was, Luke was doing a manful job of fighting, but clearly he would not prevail long. Before Penn and McCutcheon could reach the combatants, the black man shoved Luke back, came up with a pistol, and fired nearly point-blank.

Luke let out a howl.

"Nicholas Click!" Penn yelled, leveling his pistol. "Drop the gun!"

Click wheeled, glared at Penn, and fired off a quick shot. With incredible speed he vanished out the rear door of the barn and into the night.

Penn was after him right away.

McCutcheon went to Luke. "Are you shot?"

Luke was examining his torso. "I'll be . . . he missed me!" Luke laughed. "He *missed* me! God be praised!"

"Stay put," McCutcheon told him. He started to run out.

"Wait . . . where is Mack, and Joe . . . ?"

"Dead, Luke. Click murdered them both. But maybe the women and Jeremy escaped."

"They ran out . . . I saw them. They ran into the woods."

And then McCutcheon was out the rear door, into the woods himself. He was full of fury and the desire to catch the wicked Nicholas Click, but he wasn't even sure which way to run.

Jake Penn's luck had been better. He'd caught a fleeting glimpse of Click and managed to stay on his trail. He had no idea whether Click was running toward a particular destination, or simply blindly fleeing. Either way he intended to stay upon him.

This man had murdered innocent people because of their heritage. This man had married

Penn's own sister and abused her. Penn would not let him escape.

He pressed on, using his ears even more than his eyes to keep on Click's trail. He ran recklessly, ignoring the risks of ankle-grabbing roots and eye-poking branches. He would not let this man escape.

Susanna had thrown off her sling and was not even aware of the pain in her arm as she ran along, holding on to Jeremy's hand and imploring him to keep up. Marie was so terrified that she made no sound except loud and repetitive gasps.

They had run out of hell but felt like it was still just behind them.

The horror had begun without warning, the murderer and Joe Tifton grappling together, bursting through the door. Joe might have prevailed had not the killer gotten his hands on the fireplace poker. Poor, brave Joe! Susanna hoped he was alive, but she feared the worst.

The worst of it was leaving her father there helpless. She had no choice. Marie was helpless by nature, Jeremy just a boy. Both had to be taken out of the house right away . . . it's what Mack would have told her to do had he been able.

She was sure her father was dead. She hoped he had died without suffering and prayed for his soul.

Jeremy was sputtering, weeping. "Hush!" she ordered. "Hush!"

"Got to . . . stop . . ." Marie gasped.

Susanna knew she was right. They had run hard and far and could not go longer. Susanna saw a knoll ahead to the right.

"Behind there," she said. "We'll hide."

They ran around the knoll and dropped into a recess in the rocks. Jeremy sobbed and Marie continued gasping as if still running.

"Try to be quiet," Susanna urged in a whisper. "Be quiet, and pray, in your minds. Pray hard."

She wished she had a weapon. She'd run out of the house with nothing in hand. She did not even have her coat, and it was very cold.

Susanna listened to the forest behind her. She heard the sound of running feet drawing nearer.

They would be discovered. She was sure of it. Without hesitation she did what she knew her father would do, and pulled away from the others. "Stay here," she ordered, and then ran. She would lure the pursuer away, keep the others safe first and worry about herself second.

She heard him but still did not see him. Darting through the woods, she put distance between herself and where Marie and Jeremy hid. She ran until her heart felt it would burst, then slowed down because she had no choice.

Susanna stood panting, too tired to go on and no longer sure where she was.

She heard him then, pounding up close behind her. She turned; his arm swept up and around her neck. She felt the cold blade of a knife pressing against her throat as she was swept around.

"Stop!" her captor shouted into the forest. "I'll kill her, I'll cut her head off right here!"

She saw a second man come into view. Little of him was visible, but when he spoke she realized that he, like her captor, was a black man.

"Let her go, Click. Let her go. You don't want to hurt her."

"You ain't going to kill me!" Click said.

"If you stab her, I will kill you. It will do you no good at all to hurt her, because that will only assure your own death."

"Who are you?"

"My name is Jake Penn. I'm Nora's brother, Click."

"The hell you say . . ."

"Let her go. Then you and me can settle this like men."

"I'll not let you kill me!"

"You want to die, Click. Nobody does what you've done who doesn't want to die. You were a wicked man, a thief, a wife-beater, maybe worse. You talk about vengeance for Nora, but all you're really doing is trying to get somebody else to do what you're too big a coward to do yourself: end your worthless life." Penn was making it up as he went along. He had no notion of what motivated a man such as Click. The point was to keep the conversation going and hope that McCutcheon would show up.

Click turned his attention to Susanna. "You're a Caywood, ain't you."

Susanna did not answer.

"You're a Caywood . . . I'm going to kill you like I killed the others. In vengeance for Nora."

Jake Penn heard something. He looked past Click and Susanna.

Something was happening in the woods behind Click. Movement, massive movement.

From the woods emerged armed horsemen. Fifteen or more of them. Click wheeled, facing them, the knife still at Susanna's throat.

"Who the hell are you?" Click demanded.

Susanna knew them. These were Harpers. She did not yet know that these very men had earlier in the night taken the life of her cousin Ben in ambush, but she did know that the man who held her had killed Harpers as well as Caywoods.

Quick as lightning she pulled herself down and to the side, twisting out of Click's arms before he could react.

"He's the murderer!" she screamed. "He's the one!"

She scrambled away, toward Jake Penn, a man she did not know but whom she trusted because he had tried to save her. He took her arm and they ran together, leaving the Harpers and Click behind.

The horsemen moved up and in, surrounding the lone man. He glared at their mostly unseen faces.

Penn and Susanna were on the far side of the ridge from the Harpers when they heard the explosion of shots. Fifteen rifles fired as one, aimed at a single target.

Chapter Thirty-three

Two weeks later

Jake Penn filled his pipe slowly, tamping the tobacco evenly into place and lighting it carefully. He blew out a fragrant cloud of smoke and watched it drift out from under Mack Caywood's porch.

The door opened and Susanna emerged, her eyes wet. She quickly dried them when she saw Penn there, forcing out a smile.

Penn smiled back. *Strong-willed woman*, he thought. *Never willing to let any weakness show through.*

"I like the smell of your pipe," she commented.

"Yes, ma'am. I've always enjoyed that smell myself."

She nodded and stared across the yard, watching her uncle Luke pacing back and forth over by the creek. Back and forth, in endless motion, his hand occasionally waving as he spoke to himself or perhaps to no one at all. He had been a troubled man already. Now he seemed increasingly less a part of the world around him and more lost in his own guilt-ridden mind.

"Life is a strange thing," Penn observed quietly. "A mixture of tragedy and miracles. We've seen both here, no question about it."

She looked at Penn. "I'm so sorry that it was tragedy for you. Jim told me that you've been searching for your sister for years. I'm very sorry that you had to discover that she is gone."

"I always knew it was a possibility that I'd find she was dead," Penn replied. "So I guess I was at least a little ready for the news when it came. My tragedy is small compared to what you've had to suffer."

From inside the house came a cough and an immediate yell of pain. Susanna smiled to hear it, though. "If we've had tragedy, we've also had the miracle. And a miracle it is that Pap is still living."

"Indeed, ma'am. Jim and I both believed he had died right in our presence. To be as sick as he was and then to be stabbed . . . It truly was a miracle he lived."

"Right now living is something of a torment for him, though. Every cough makes the stab wound hurt. What hurts even worse is his grief for Ben. And for poor Joe Tifton, too. I think it hurts him to know that Joe died trying to defend him after he'd been so harsh with him."

"It's Deborah who bears the worst of that, though," Penn said. "Apparently she truly loved that young man."

"She did. It saddens me so much to see the transformation that has happened. You didn't know her before, Mr. Penn. Full of life and fun and spirit . . . and now she just sits and weeps. She's more like Marie than herself now."

"How's Jeremy?"

Susanna shook her head. "I don't know . . . only God knows." With the help of a local clergyman, the boy had already been sent away to a facility at the state capital to begin learning to deal with the damage that had been done to him by the horrors to which he had been exposed. No one yet knew how well he would respond.

The least changed by the ordeal was Marie. Ironically, the fact that she was perpetually glum and pessimistic and sorrowful allowed her to absorb her new griefs more easily than most. For her the tragedies were simple confirmation of a dark world view she'd held for years.

Susanna herself remained strong and stubbornly resilient, but tears came easily, and she had the look of a person wrung dry. Yet she kept going, holding together her ruined family, and Penn admired her for it.

"Let me ask you something, miss," he said.

"Do you believe that what has happened has ended the feud?"

"I do. I don't fully understand why it has done it, but it seems to have taken the fire out of it all, on both sides."

"I think I know why," Penn said. "I think it's because what happened to Nora happened because of something done by both sides. And so the revenge of her husband struck both sides as well. Even after houses being burned and men being ambushed and all that, this thing gave both sides a common enemy. Once they learned that the killer hadn't been sent against them by the other side after all, it was a little harder to hate quite so fiercely."

"The Caywoods and the Harpers will never be friends," she observed.

"No . . . but maybe they'll be slower to throw accusations at one another," Penn said. "Not to mention bullets."

"Both sides have much to be ashamed of. Ben and Luke and all of them should never have gone on that arson rampage . . . and the Harpers should never have set up an ambush."

"From their point of view, they were trying to save another Harper home from being burned."

"I know. That's the trouble with feuds. There are always grounds available for outrage, if you're determined to find them. Always something to justify stupidity and violence."

Penn sat smoking in silence as Susanna stared across the yard at the fresh grave holding the body of Ben Caywood. It was beside the grave of Ben's father, Tom, a grave scarcely much older.

"I wonder how long it will be until Jim gets back?" she asked.

Penn wondered just how much she knew about the purpose of Jim McCutcheon's trip back to Texas to see Emily Pike. He'd left shortly after Ben's burial, promising to return. Jake Penn had stayed behind to help the family in its time of difficulty and to provide some protection should it be needed. So far, it hadn't been.

Penn knew why McCutcheon had gone back to Texas. He was going to tell the truth to Emily Pike, and end their engagement. Then he would return and try to win the heart of Susanna Caywood.

Penn's intuitions, usually accurate, told him that McCutcheon already had her heart and just didn't quite know it yet.

"I expect he'll be back any time now," Penn replied.

Inside, Mack coughed and yelled in pain again. Susanna turned and went back into the house.

Penn let his pipe grow cold, tilted down his hat brim, and dozed on the porch. An hour later he opened his eyes, pushed the brim back up again, and looked into the grinning face of Jim McCutcheon, freshly arrived back from Texas.

"Dang it . . . I'd hoped to come poke you in the side while you were still asleep and see how high you'd jump," McCutcheon said.

"I'd have come up shooting," Penn replied. "I've probably killed thirty or forty men who poked me while I was sleeping."

"Yeah, I'm sure," McCutcheon replied. He stuck out his hand and shook Penn's. "Good to be back with you again, Penn."

"How'd it go in Texas?"

McCutcheon laughed, reached into his pocket, and pulled out an engagement ring. "She had it off and ready to give back to me even before I got there to ask for it," he said. "Seems that in my absence, her former husband showed up out of the blue. Declared himself a changed man, and apparently gave them cause to believe he really is. Little Martin was tickled to death to have his real pa with him. Anyway, it appears that Emily still plans to get married . . . just not to me."

"Durn, Jim, that's a peculiar twist of events. I feel like I ought to tell you how sorry I am and congratulate you all at the same time."

"It was a good thing, Penn. I was able to act sorrowful but dignified and supportive all at once. And now I've got my ring back . . . in hopes that I can give it away again real soon."

"It was like I was telling Susanna a little while ago: There's miracles and tragedy all mixed together in this old life. Bad things come, and good things with them."

"Ain't that the truth." McCutcheon cast a meaningful glance over his shoulder.

Penn followed his gaze and saw a figure standing at the end of the road leading up to the Caywood house. A black woman, simply but nicely dressed, standing in a posture that signified both dignity and nervousness.

Penn rose and gazed at her, knowing it was probably a rude-looking stare but finding himself unable to tear his eyes away. Even across this distance there was something about her . . .

"Jim . . . who is that?"

McCutcheon was grinning even more broadly now. "Let me tell you something, Jake: There's more folks than you and me who read that newspaper story about the killer. There's more folks than you and me who saw a significance in that phrase 'Vengeance for Nora.' There's more folks than you and me who decided to come investigate for themselves. You and me just got here faster. That one out there"—he tilted his head back toward the woman—"just didn't get here as quick as you and I did."

"Jim, are you telling me that . . . Are you saying that . . ." Penn faltered away, unable to get out his words.

"Let me tell you a brief little story, Penn, about the history of this area. There was once a woman named Nora who lived here. She had a husband who was cruel to her, but she herself was good and tenderhearted, and did what she could to help those who were downtrodden and hurting. One of those was a sad young black woman, poor and with no choice but to sell herself into prostitution just to stay alive, who Nora fed and clothed and helped. Nora even took the only piece of jewelry she had—a bracelet—and gave it to this sad young lady. That sad young lady, unfortunately, came to a tragic end, burned to death in a barn fire . . . wearing Nora's bracelet. And Nora saw at last an opportunity to get away from a cruel husband once and for all. A way that could get her free without him ever looking for her, for he would think that she was dead."

Penn bit his lip. His eyes were growing moist as he continued to stare at the woman.

"She didn't die in that barn fire, Penn, like Luke Caywood thought, like everybody—even Nicholas Click—thought. She just fled her husband, that's all, and let everyone believe she was dead so that he'd never come after her again. She didn't know that one day the madness in him would make him come back here and begin killing to avenge the wife he thought had been murdered. But when she read a story in a newspaper that told about the killing, she figured out who was doing it, and she did the right thing. She came back, to reveal the truth."

Penn's face was streaked with tears. "It's Nora. You've brought Nora to me."

"I met her at the train station, Penn. You know how I knew her? Because she looks so much like you. When I told her you were here, and that you'd spent all these years looking for her, she cried. Bawled like a child. You see, she's never forgot you, either. And she's prayed every day of her life that someday you and she would be brought back together. And now, here you are."

Penn broke away from McCutcheon and began walking toward the sister he'd spent his life looking for. His shoulders heaved as he sobbed despite his best effort to control it. Halfway to her, his fast walk turned into a run. By then, Nora was heading toward him, too.

Susanna came out onto the porch. "Jim!" She ran to him and threw her arms around him, and kissed his cheek before she remembered that she was cool and dignified Susanna Caywood, who did not perform such displays.

McCutcheon's reply was to pull her even closer and kiss her squarely on the lips.

She did not protest. But when she pulled her face away, she nodded toward Penn and Nora, now embracing in the midst of the long drive.

"What's all this about?" she asked.

"Miracles amidst tragedy, Susanna. That's what. Good amidst the bad. And a good man's dreams coming true after many long years and long miles."

JUDSON GRAY

RANSOM RIDERS
0-451-20418-2

When Penn and McCutcheon are ambushed on their
way to rescue a millionaire's kidnapped niece, they
start to fear that the kidnapping was an inside job.

DOWN TO MARROWBONE
0-451-20158-2

Jim McCutcheon had squandered his Southern family's
fortune and had to find a way to rebuild it among the
boomtowns.

Jake Penn had escaped the bonds of slavery and had to
find his long-lost sister...

Together, they're an unlikely team—but with danger
down every trail, nothing's worth more than a friend
you can count on...

To order call: 1-800-788-6262